#9

Season of Surprises

THE MITCHELL BROTHERS SERIES

#9
Season of Surprises

THE MITCHELL BROTHERS SERIES

Brian
McFarlane

Fenn Publishing Company Ltd.
Bolton, Canada

SEASON OF SURPRISES
BOOK NINE IN THE MITCHELL BROTHERS SERIES
A Fenn Publishing Book / First Published in 2005

Fenn Publishing Company Ltd.
Bolton, Ontario, Canada

Distributed in Canada by H.B. Fenn and Company Ltd.
Bolton, Ontario, Canada, L7E 1W2
www.hbfenn.com

Library and Archives Canada Cataloguing in Publication

McFarlane, Brian, 1931-
        Season of surprises / Brian McFarlane.

(The Mitchell Brothers series ; 9)
For ages 8-12.
ISBN 1-55168-300-8

I. Title. II. Series.
PS8575.F37S42 2005   jC813'.54   C2005-904685-6

SEASON OF SURPRISES

NOTE FROM THE AUTHOR

The Indian River hockey team needs help. What the club doesn't need is a figure skater from England, a centreman who joins the roster when his wealthy aunt, the team owner, insists he be included. Coach Kennedy and brothers Max and Marty Mitchell, the teenage stars of the team, must find a way to win games despite front-office shenanigans, some unlikely recruits and the softy at centre. They hope their efforts will overcome setbacks and eventually bring success—on and off the ice—especially during a memorable cloak-and-dagger trip to Europe.

Brian McFarlane

CHAPTER 1

A NEW HOCKEY SEASON

The dozen or so Indian River fans watching the practice session at rinkside greeted 17-year-old Max Mitchell with a mixture of "oohs" and "aahs" as he completed a dazzling rush up the ice.

Max, first-string centre on the hometown junior hockey team, the Indians, drew a defenceman out of position by faking a pass, swooped around him and stormed in on goal. He looked up, held his shot, forced the goaltender to slide out to meet him and deftly slipped the puck into the open corner of the net.

"You bum!" shouted the goalie, slamming his stick on the ice. "You couldn't do that again in a million years." The angry reaction made Max laugh out loud. The goalie was his younger brother, Marty.

Max was still laughing when he circled back toward the goal. "Better learn to cut down those angles, brother," he admonished. "If you don't, you'll never make it to the NHL."

Coach Steve Kennedy, standing behind the

1

home team's bench, nodded in approval at Max Mitchell's play. He thought: *This kid is a natural. There's no telling how far he might go in hockey. That's one reason I enjoy coaching young men. Every so often you get a kid who can do it all. And when you get a kid like that who has heart, a real passion for the game—like young Mitchell—well, it's just a pleasure to be around such an individual. And you know, his kid brother Marty isn't bad, either. He's got spunk. Going to be a fine goalie some day.*

Kennedy liked to quote proverbs, and the players he coached loved hearing them. If a player boastfully predicted that he'd score 30 goals, Kennedy might say, "Remember, son, between saying and doing, many a pair of skates can be worn out."

When a player fouled up on the ice, Kennedy would bark, "Wake up! Your head is not just for growing hair."

A player late for an early morning practice might hear Kennedy sigh and say, "A lazy boy and a warm bed are difficult to part."

As he watched Max Mitchell at work on the ice, and saw his potential, he said to himself, "He's got to do his own growing, no matter how tall his grandfather was."

Then Steve Kennedy looked at his watch, and thought: *These fellows will scrimmage until midnight if I let them. But for some—like the Mitchells—there's school tomorrow, and homework to be done. Others have to be at the paper mill for the early shift. There are plenty of sacrifices to be made if you're an aspiring hockey player these days. Or a coach.*

He blew his whistle. "That's it for today, fellows," he shouted. "Take three laps around the rink and you're through."

With Max leading the way, the Indians skated the laps. Max loved the joy of skating. His boots were a good fit, his blades recently sharpened, his body trim and muscular. He loved to hear the scruntch, scruntch, scruntch of sharp steel blades on hard ice. He remembered those sounds from his childhood, when his father and mother had built a small rink for their sons in the backyard. Harry and Amy Mitchell had first met at a hockey game. He was a young sports reporter; she was the star player on the Snowflakes, the best women's hockey team in the North Country. His parents' skates had made the same sound as they taught Max and Marty the fundamentals of the game.

Thanks, Mom and Dad, Max thought, *for showing me the joys of hockey. I hope to play this game until I'm 90. Maybe even 100.*

Max had blond hair and blue eyes, weighed in at 180 pounds and was a shade over six feet. "Ideal size and weight for a hockey forward,"

Coach Kennedy had told him. "Most of the 1936 Montreal team—the Stanley Cup champs last season—are about that size."

Max cut in sharply behind the net, then accelerated, putting distance between himself and his teammates. His hair flew back in the breeze created by his speed. Suddenly he felt a surprise whack on his butt. He turned to see his brother Marty, two years younger and two inches shorter, waving his big goal stick.

"I'll whack you again if you keep showing me up in practice," Marty said with a grin. "You scored three times on me today. You're trying to cost me my job!"

Max laughed, aware that Marty had cut across the ice to slide in behind him. He slowed his pace so Marty could catch up.

"You don't have to worry, Marty. Coach Kennedy likes you. Just concentrate on those angles. And when a forward breaks in on you, always try to get him to make the first move."

"I'll be glad when the season starts," Marty sighed. "Then I won't have to face you in practice anymore."

"I can hardly wait," Max replied. "A new season always brings a whole lot of surprises—especially in junior hockey. I know one thing—it'll be hard to win the Northern League championship again. We're not nearly as strong as last year."

"It's not so hard to win if a team has great goal-tending," Marty offered. "That's what I'm here for." He sighed again. "Of course, I seldom get the respect I deserve—the appreciation, the honours, the awards. My big brother nails down most of those. Oh well, goalies have always had to suffer in silence."

Max showed little sympathy. He said, "You poor kid—you're about as silent as a brass band. Remember what Coach Kennedy said, 'The dog that barks all the time gets little attention.'" Max was accustomed to Marty's mock complaints. And his chatter.

"You give up fewer than three goals a game this season and come up with a few shutouts and you'll get plenty of respect," he added. "Consider yourself lucky to be playing junior at your age. Not many kids do."

"Really? I've been ready for junior since I was ten or 11," Marty bragged. "It's just that nobody else thought I was ready—or big enough. Well, let's go in. I want to get these pads off."

"I'll say one thing. You've never lacked confidence," Max said, throwing an arm around Marty. "That's a sign of a good goalie."

When they stepped off the ice, a young fan greeted them. Charlie Chin was the 15-year-old son of the owner of the town's only Chinese restaurant, the Golden Dragon. He slapped Marty on the back with his arm and said, "Hello, Mitchells. You're looking good out there. Ready for another good season?"

"Hi, Charlie," said Max. "Nobody comes to more practices and games than you do." He shrugged off a glove. "Give me five, pal."

"Aw, you don't want to shake hands with me," replied their slim friend. He shyly slipped his right hand behind his back.

"Give it here," Max demanded. He held out his own right hand. "Come on, Charlie. I'm your pal."

Slowly, Charlie Chin extended his hand, a hand made useless months earlier during a careless, horrifying moment. He had been lighting giant firecrackers in his backyard. One exploded when lit, shooting flames and powder into his hand, burning the flesh to the bone. Surgeons had tried to save his hand, but infection had set in and most of it had been amputated. Now a metal clamp attached to Charlie's wrist reflected the arena lights.

Max grasped the cold metal and gave it a quick shake. "No need to be embarrassed, Charlie," he said. "The loss of your hand doesn't make you less of a person."

"Aw, I know, Max," Charlie replied. "It's just that my new hand is so...so ugly." He grimaced. "And I can't play hockey anymore. I was hoping to play with you and Marty someday."

"You can play soccer, Charlie," Marty said, nudging his friend with an elbow. "Or baseball. A one-armed player once made it all the way to the major leagues."

"You can run on the track team," Max added. "You're really fast."

"I was hoping I could be the Indians' stick boy this season," Charlie said, his eyes brightening. "Or maybe an assistant trainer."

"Hey, that's a good idea," Max said. "Except we don't have a trainer for you to assist. Let's go see the coach. I'm sure he'll fit you in somewhere."

The brothers, with Charlie in tow, clumped down the corridor and into the Indians' dressing room.

Prominently displayed on one wall of the room was a photo of last season's team. The 1935 champions had overcome many obstacles in their run to the junior title. First, the crusty owner of the Gray Paper Mill in town decided that hockey was no longer worthy of his sponsorship. Then their coach, accountant Steve Kennedy, had been transferred to the mill's Chatsworth plant. When rental costs for the arena ice became prohibitive, Max, as player-coach, had organized an outdoor game—on the river ice. He had recruited a player from the Tumbling Waters Indian reserve—Sammy Running Fox—to bolster his team. And he'd called on his kid brother Marty to substitute in goal when the team's regular netminder had refused to play with Sammy. Fan support swelled when Max moulded this unlikely group of teenagers into a winning combination.

Now the Indians were back—this time with the support of the paper mill and with the highly respected Steve Kennedy recalled from Chatsworth to mentor the players.

But Kennedy had already spotted some glaring weaknesses in this season's team. Aside from Max, they had nobody who could play centre. Without a solid number-two pivot, a skilled play-maker, his team's chances of repeating as junior champs were extremely slim. Also, the Indians lacked depth. Kennedy was frantically trying to find enough talent to form a third line.

The coach greeted Charlie Chin warmly. "Max tells me you were a fine hockey player until your...your accident," he said. "Max said when your parents came to the North Country they changed your name to Charlie after Charlie Conacher, the great right winger for the Toronto Maple Leafs."

Charlie laughed. "Nobody could have pronounced my Chinese name," he said. "And I love the name Charlie. It's a good hockey name."

"We need all the help we can get," the coach told the youngster. "We'll certainly make you stick boy. Better still, I'll make you my assistant. You can look after a lot of the detail work I don't have time for."

"Like what, Mr. Kennedy?" Charlie asked.

"Like travel arrangements for road games. And scheduling—practice times and that sort of thing. You can buy new pucks and sticks when we need them. You can fill water bottles and make sure the jerseys and socks get cleaned every so often. During games, you can keep statistics." He leaned closer, not wanting the others to hear. "Will you do it for five bucks a week? We don't have a big budget. I'll pay you out of my own pocket."

"Heck, I'll do it for nothing," said Charlie. "Thanks, Mr. Kennedy. You don't know what it means to me to be with your hockey club."

Kennedy said, "It's the next best thing to playing. The Mitchell brothers tell me you're the smartest kid in school. And a hard worker, too. I see you mastered English in no time at all. So welcome aboard."

The coach extended a hand and Charlie hesitated, then placed the metal attachment to his arm in Kennedy's big mitt.

Charlie Chin was ecstatic. He shrugged out of his jacket and scurried around the dressing room, greeting old friends. Then he began picking up bits of tape and gum wrappers from the floor and placing sticks back in the stick rack.

Later, outside the dressing room door, the

coach huddled with James Taylor, the president of the hockey club. Taylor worked for the Gray Paper Mill and fancied himself a hockey expert. After the recent death of the mill owner, Mrs. Gray, the owner's widow, had appointed Taylor to make all of the major decisions involving the mill—and the hockey team. Her son Johnny might easily have filled the role, but he was a student athlete at Yale, studying to be a lawyer.

With the season opener a week away, Taylor had come out to look over the talent on the team.

"What do you think, Mr. Taylor?" asked Kennedy.

"I like the way Max Mitchell's performing," Taylor replied. "He's even faster than last season. And the kid we recruited off the Tumbling Waters reserve last year, Sammy Fox, looks sharp. Kelly Jackson is a solid winger. All local kids, too, which means a lot of friends and families at every home game."

"And the goaltending?"

"Marty's young, but he moves fast in goal, doesn't he? All in all, it looks like a pretty good club. And the defencemen are pretty solid."

"Mr. Taylor, you brought in three new imports this year—Oliver and Riddell, and Cassidy, the defenceman. That's all each team is allowed. I'm worried about how they'll fit in."

"They'll fit like a glove," Taylor replied sharply.

"I scouted them personally, and I signed them. I pride myself in knowing talent when I see it."

"They haven't gone out of their way to make friends with their new teammates," observed Kennedy.

"They'll be fine," Taylor replied. "Give them time. They're probably just shy."

"Oh, they're not shy," Kennedy said. "Quite the opposite. If anything, they think quite highly of themselves. Oliver thinks he should be on the first line—ahead of Fox and Jackson. No way."

"Well, we were lucky to get them. You know Mrs. Gray won't tolerate paying players. She lets me find good jobs for them in the mill, but hockey salaries—no. The three I recruited have all finished high school, so they're happy to be here in Indian River."

Steve Kennedy wasn't so sure. He didn't tell Mr. Taylor he'd seen some evidence of unhappiness among the three newcomers. There'd been some grumbling in the dressing room about "second-rate equipment" and the "hayseed fans" who attended the workouts.

Kennedy had tried to straighten them out.

"The equipment is the best we can afford," he had told them. "Sure, some of the pads are a couple of years old. Get used to wearing them—this isn't the NHL. And those hayseeds who support us are the best dern fans in the world. Don't ever let me hear you knocking them."

Taylor took a sip from his paper coffee cup and said to the coach, "Only one thing concerns me—the lack of depth. We don't have a solid third line."

"It concerns me, too," Kennedy said. "There just aren't any more kids in Indian River who can do the job. We've tried them all."

"Fortunately I brought you a good centreman in Ollie Oliver. And a top winger in Hack Riddell. They're both first-rate."

"No, they're not," Kennedy said bluntly. "Oliver is not a natural centre. He's not a playmaker. Hasn't shown much so far. I'm going to try him on left wing. And Riddell is selfish with the puck. They're flashy, maybe, but neither one has shown me any leadership qualities. At least Cassidy seems like a decent defenceman."

Taylor was taken aback. He had more or less promised Oliver that he'd be the second-line centre on the team. And now this. "Well then, what about Elmo Swift," he asked, "the other lad from the Tumbling Waters reserve? We had great luck with Sammy Fox, the player Max discovered last season."

"Don't know yet, Mr. Taylor," Kennedy said. "Fox established himself quickly and became a star. Elmo Swift is a different breed—if you'll pardon the expression. He's improving but he's still finding himself. Right now he's a third-stringer. Guess we'll just have to pray that someone picks his game up a notch and grabs that opening at centre on the second line.

"The good news is," he added, "we've found ourselves a stick boy, trainer, statistician and assistant coach—all in one. Young Charlie Chin has volunteered to help out."

"The Chinese kid?" Mr. Taylor asked. "He was a good player himself until he had that dreadful accident. He'll never play again."

"Well, he's with us now. Being surrounded by fellows his own age may help him to get over the loss of his hand."

James Taylor punched Steve Kennedy lightly on the chest with a gloved hand. "You're the best coach in the Northern League," he said, "and we hope you'll be around for years to come. I'm sure you'll find the answer to our problem at centre."

Now Kennedy paused. He thought: *What's all this about "hoping" I'll be around? Didn't sound much like a vote of confidence to me. Maybe Taylor has someone else in mind for my job. More likely he has his eye on it for himself.*

He remembered Taylor as a player in a minor pro league a decade earlier. He was a self-centred performer, always checking on his personal goals and assists. If he was on the ice after his team scored, Taylor would tell the referee, "That was mine, Ref" or "I set that one up, Ref—don't forget my assist."

Conversely, when he was in a defensive role, he would chirp, "I had my man," when he came to the bench after his team gave up a goal. As a result, his teammates began calling him Mountie. When someone had asked why, they were told, "Don't you get it? Mounties always get their man."

Taylor said, "Coach, Mrs. Gray would like you to stop by her house tonight. Says she has something important to talk to you about."

When Kennedy frowned and said, "Uh oh," Taylor gripped him by the arm. "It's nothing to worry about. In fact, Mrs. Gray says you'll be delighted with what she has to tell you. Oh, she said to bring the team captain with you. And his kid brother if you like."

Mrs. Gray was the widow of Harry Edison Gray, founder of the Gray Paper Mill, a prosperous company that was the town's only real industry. For years, Mr. Gray had felt it was important to contribute several hundred dollars each year to sponsor the junior hockey club. And with Max leading the way, they had proven the year before that they deserved it. After her husband's recent death, Mrs. Gray had decided to carry on the tradition.

"Why in the world would Mrs. Gray want to see the Mitchell brothers and me?" Kennedy asked.

Taylor gave him a mysterious smile. "You'll find out," he said. He tapped Kennedy on the arm and walked away.

Coaching hockey meant a lot to Steve Kennedy. He enjoyed his job in the accounting department at the mill, but his favourite place to be was on the rink, teaching the skills of the game, motivating young players, hopefully moulding a team of winners.

But each season brought a new set of problems. As he switched off the lights and closed the dressing room door, Steve had a hunch he was about to encounter a major one.

CHAPTER 2

MRS. GRAY'S BIG SURPRISE

Mrs. Gray was a pleasant, old-fashioned little woman who lived in a pleasant, old-fashioned little house on the hill that overlooked the pleasant, old-fashioned little town. She had moved into the house recently, after her husband passed away and her two children went off to college.

Her house was painted grey, the fence around it was grey and the doghouse in the yard was grey.

"I'll bet you I know what kind of dog she owns," Marty said, smiling.

"What kind?" asked Max.

"A greyhound, of course." Marty chuckled at his own joke.

"Could you be serious for the next hour or so?" Max suggested.

It was impossible to dislike Mrs. Gray, because she took pride in knowing every man, woman, child, dog and cat in Indian River. She had a heart the size of a giant pumpkin, and she generously supported every bake sale and church social and

16

all of the numerous fundraisers in the community.

"Come in, gentlemen, come in," she greeted Steve Kennedy and the Mitchell brothers when she met them at her door. When she took their coats and began hanging them on an old-fashioned coat rack in the vestibule, Marty nudged Max and whispered, "See the dress she has on? It's grey. And her hair is grey. Just like the carpet and the walls."

"Hush," said Max, poking Marty in the ribs.

Just then, a small dog, a Pekinese, poked its head into the vestibule, and Marty almost burst out laughing. It too, was grey.

Mrs. Gray gave Marty a puzzled look, and then said, "I have tea and cookies waiting for you in the parlour. Max and Marty, how are your parents? Your mother is such a charming woman. And your father is doing such a good job running the local newspaper." She noted that her visitors had unlaced and removed their shoes.

"Thank you for being so considerate," she said. "I try to keep my floors clean but it's so difficult at this time of year. Now let's go into the parlour."

Max and Steve stopped short when they entered the room. A strange-looking young man awaited them there. He was tall and slim, with slicked-back blond hair. A small blond moustache was perched on his upper lip. He rose to greet them and extended a pink hand. He wore a pinstriped navy blue suit like the one the bank manager or the undertaker in town might wear, polished brown shoes and a dazzling yellow tie. And his shirtsleeves ended in gold cuff links. His nails were manicured, and both Max and Steve sniffed the air, their nostrils tickled by the young man's fragrant after-shave lotion. The aroma was so strong that Max began to sneeze.

"Pardon me," he said, waving a hand in front of his face. "Must be my allergies."

While Max sneezed, Marty reached for the cookies and devoured two in record time.

"This," said Mrs. Gray proudly, "is my nephew from England—Clarence Clarington-Clarke."

Steve Kennedy gripped the stranger by the hand. He had no idea Mrs. Gray had relatives in England. "Pleased to meet you, Clarence," he said. "Welcome to the North Country. I'm sorry, what was your last name again?"

"Clarington-Clarke," said Clarence, flashing a toothy grin. "With a hyphen. And with an 'e' on the end of Clarke."

"Well, that's a...a...mouthful," said Kennedy.

Max stepped forward, "Nice to meet you, Clarence," he said. "Are you planning to stay in Indian River long?"

"For as long as Auntie will have me," the young man replied, chuckling. "I have always like snowy things, icy things, you know, and what better place to find them than in the North Country. I plan to stay until summer time, old chap. Perhaps longer."

"Clarence loves North America," Mrs. Gray interrupted. "Before I invited him here, he spent some time with relatives in Boston and Montreal. He enjoys winter sports, and he's tried most of them."

"I gave up skiing when I couldn't stop and ran into a tree," Clarence confessed. "I was spitting out bark for the next two days."

Max suppressed a grin but Marty burst out laughing.

Steve Kennedy found himself wondering what this meeting with Clarence had to do with him. He soon found out—to his horror.

"Clarence is madly in love with hockey," Mrs. Gray said. "His mother, my sister Penelope—back in England—tells me he's quite good at it. Back home he took figure skating lessons for some time and then gravitated toward hockey."

"I didn't think they played much hockey in England," Max said. He, too, wondered where all this was leading.

"It's not hugely popular," Clarence explained, "not like football—which I believe you call soccer. But some of the chaps play it. And I happen to be among the fortunate few."

"The reason we're meeting here tonight,"

Mrs. Gray said, "is because I've asked Clarence to play for our junior team—the Indians. Mr. Taylor mentioned you were short of players, Steve. I'm so pleased that Clarence has agreed. I went right downtown and bought him a new pair of skates. Isn't this a wonderful surprise?"

Steve Kennedy had raised a cup of tea halfway to his lips and came close to spilling it on the carpet. Marty was so surprised he dropped a chocolate cookie on the rug.

"It is, indeed," Kennedy stammered. "It's a big surprise. I've heard of players going from North America to England to play, but never the other way around." Inwardly, he groaned. He knew that Mrs. Gray's word was law in Indian River. If her nephew wanted to play hockey for the local team, he would play—even if he skated on his ankles and held his stick like a pool cue. Guess who paid the bills?

"Well now, Clarence," he said, studying the dapper young gentleman sitting opposite him. "What position do you play?"

"It makes no difference," Clarence replied. "All of them, I guess. All but stopper."

"Stopper?"

"Yes, goaltender. I shudder to think of playing stopper—getting hit by all those pucks. One would have to be subhuman to be a goaltender."

"That was my position when I was young,"

Steve said quietly.

"And my brother Marty is a stopper—I mean a goaltender," Max added. Marty grunted, his mouth full of cookie crumbs.

Clarence blushed. "Sorry, old chaps," he said. "Me and my big gob."

"Gob?" asked Max.

"My big mouth," Clarence explained.

"Could you play centre ice?" Max asked.

"If that's the position you have open, I shall excel at centre ice," Clarence boasted.

Mrs. Gray put down her teacup. "I'm so thrilled we have a team here in Indian River that Clarence can play on," she trilled, beaming fondly at Clarence over her spectacles. "But, Mr. Kennedy, you must see that the other players are not too rough on Clarence. He was sickly as a boy, and he's still rather, well, delicate."

Kennedy gulped. *If Clarence was sickly why didn't he play games like hide and seek?* he thought. *Or hopscotch?*

Clarence spoke up. "You mustn't worry about me, Auntie, really. I'll be quite all right. In hockey, players do run into each other by accident from time to time. It's a jolly good game."

Now Max gulped. Players not only run into each other by accident but they often try to annihilate each other—on purpose!

"Thank you for having me on your club,"

Clarence said. "I'll be willing to turn out for a practice session any time you say, old chap. I'll bring the new skates Auntie bought for me."

I should hope so, thought the coach. *The team doesn't supply skates.*

Kennedy felt ill. He couldn't afford to argue with Mrs. Gray. She could shut down all hockey in Indian River if she had a mind to. But what sort of hockey team was he going to have with the dapper Clarence as the second-string centre? Who could tell? Mrs. Gray might even decide he should be first string—ahead of Max. *She could even make him player-coach,* he thought ruefully.

He had whipped his players into shape, and now that they were ready for league play, along comes a Brit who says "jolly good" and "old chap" and "I'll be willing to come to practice any time you say."

"Our practices are in the evening," Kennedy said. "So the mill workers can get there."

"Fine with me," said Clarence. "Shall we say seven o'clock?"

"Yes, yes," said Kennedy, getting up to leave. "Seven will be fine."

"Righto, sir," Clarence assured him brightly. "I shall be there at seven. On the dot. Tallyho, gentlemen."

Max was about to reach for a cookie, but the plate was bare. He glared at Marty, who grinned back at him.

The Mitchells and their coach left the Gray house in a daze. "Now what am I gonna do, fellows?" Steve asked as he drove Max and Marty home. "First, Taylor decides on our imports. Now I'm saddled with a dude who is just too...too precious to take a bodycheck. A figure skater, for heaven's sake. A kid who talks like the Duke of Windsor. You've got to help me get rid of this pantywaist—fast. And without upsetting Mrs. Gray."

Max was silent for a moment. Then he said, "We're allowed three imports, Coach, not four. How can we possibly add Clarence to the lineup without breaking the rules?"

"Good thinking, Max. I'll check with the league office first thing in the morning. Even though no team has ever recruited a player from England, Clarence has to be considered an import. There's our out! I'll explain nicely to Mrs. Gray that her loving nephew is ineligible. I'll tell her how badly we all feel." He chuckled. "Say, I feel better already. What say we stop at Merry Mabel's for some ice cream?"

But when Steve Kennedy spoke with the league president by telephone the following morning, he was shocked to learn that the league was making an exception in the case of Clarence Clarington-Clarke.

"The import rule is for players moving between

teams in North America," Mr. Billings, the president, explained. "Nothing in the rule book about players moving here from England. It's never happened before. Anyway, I figure it'll be good publicity to have a Brit in the league. A lot of immigrants from England live in the North Country. You should be happy, Steve—maybe lots of them will come out to the games."

Steve Kennedy shook his head when he hung up.

"I'll give Clarence jersey number 13," he muttered, "and hope it brings him all kinds of bad luck."

The coach was still babbling to himself when he drove to the practice that night.

CHAPTER 3
ANGER IN THE DRESSING ROOM

There was a disturbing scene in the dressing room when Steve Kennedy told his players he was shifting his roster around to make room for a new player—Mr. Clarence Clarington-Clarke, a centre-iceman.

"What?" howled Ollie Oliver, who had just been told he was about to be shifted to right wing. James Taylor had recruited him as a centre, offering him a good job in the mill as an incentive. "Centre's *my* position, coach," he bawled. "Shift me to the wing? Nothin' doing. Taylor promised me."

"Taylor's the team president. He doesn't run the club on the ice, I do," Kennedy retorted. "I'm sorry, Ollie. You'll have to play on right wing and that's that. At least for the next little while."

"How about me?" yelped Hack Riddell. "I'm the right winger on the second line. And Ollie's my centreman."

The coach ran a hand through his thinning hair. He picked a ball of black tape off the floor and tossed it in the wastebasket.

"Listen, men, it's early," he answered, looking at Riddell. "We haven't played a game yet. But I hope to put together a third line. There'll be injuries and illness, I'm sure. For the moment, Hack, you'll be a utility forward."

"Utility forward!" Riddell snorted. "I know what that means. I don't get on the ice at all unless somebody breaks his leg or gets the flu. Nuts to that!" He threw his gloves on the floor in disgust.

Oliver followed suit, throwing his gloves into his hockey bag. "I knew something like this would happen when I came to this bush-league town," he said bitterly. "Well, I won't stand for it. I play centre or I don't play at all."

The other members of the team had never seen such a display of temper. It amounted to a mutiny. They waited to see how their coach would handle this confrontation.

Kennedy knew what to do.

"Then that's it," he said flatly. "You boys can turn in your uniforms. We'll just have to get along without you. Clarence plays second-line centre whether you like it or not. But you know what I think you fellows should do? Stick around. See what happens. Hockey is full of surprises. Who knows? Mr. Clarington-Clarke may get homesick for England and be gone in a few days."

Oliver sank down on a bench and put his head

in his hands. He knew it would be difficult to get a transfer to another team at this late date. And he enjoyed his cushy job at the mill. Because he was a hockey player, the foreman gave him special privileges. After a few rebellious mutterings he started to climb into his hockey gear.

Hack Riddell, however, put on his coat and started for the door.

"Walk out and you needn't come back," Kennedy reminded him quietly.

Riddell hesitated. "Coach, I came here to play hockey. Not to sit around as a bloomin' utility man—keepin' the bench warm for the other guys."

"Listen, Hack, I told you I'm doing the best I can. At the moment we're a two-line team. I'd like to form a third line, but we're a couple of players short. Stick with me and maybe you'll get more hockey than you ever imagined you would."

At that moment, the door flew open. Through the portal stepped Clarence Clarington-Clarke. He wore a long beige coat with a fur collar, a gorgeous silk scarf, a brown fedora and yellow gloves.

"Good evening, chaps," he greeted his new teammates. "Sorry to be a bit tardy. I had a wee bit of trouble locating the stadium."

It was the first time any of the Indian River boys had heard their old rink called a stadium. Some of them snickered.

The others responded to Clarence's cheery

greeting with grunts, barely acknowledging his arrival.

Wanting to be welcoming, Max said, "There's a place over here," and pointed to a spot on the bench beside him.

"Jolly good," said Clarence, striding across the room and sliding out of his overcoat.

"Would your valet be kind enough to take my overcoat and place it in your cloakroom?" he asked Max.

Max grinned. "Clarence, there's a hook over your place on the bench. Clothes go on the hook, shoes go under the bench. We don't have a cloak-room."

"And we haven't hired a valet yet," Marty piped up, making everybody laugh—including Clarence.

Kennedy introduced Clarence all around. "Hello, hello, hello," he said agreeably, as players shook hands with him quickly—as if they were happy to get the ritual over with.

It was obvious Clarence was an interloper, an outsider who was only on the club because of his relationship to Mrs. Gray. The Indians wanted no part of him.

But the frigid reception he received didn't bother Clarence in the least.

He nudged Max with a hard elbow. "I expect I'll be a little rusty at first. The hockey we played in England might be different from what you play

here. I'd be most grateful, old chap, for any point-
ers you might give me."

"What are your strong points, Clarence?" Max
asked.

"Well, my forte is skating, of course—from my
figure skating days. And my dribbling should be
quite good."

In the corner, Marty was strapping on his pads.
"Dribbling?" he snorted. "What's dribbling? And
what's forte?"

"Sorry," Clarence explained. "By dribbling I
meant my stickhandling. Dribbling is a football—
sorry, soccer—phrase. And my forte means my
best skill."

"My dad just turned 40," Sammy Fox quipped.

Max caught a couple of his teammates rolling
their eyes at Clarence.

Two burly defencemen, Cassidy and Leblanc,
began whispering to each other. They were cook-
ing something up, Max could tell.

When Clarence got changed, Max noticed that
he was more muscular than he would have imagined. And his handshake had been surprisingly
firm.

*Now if he'd only shave off that silly moustache
and wash the grease out of hair,* Max thought, *he
would look all right—almost normal.*

Kennedy had enough regulars and spares for
two teams—red shirts versus whites. Some of the

spares were high-school kids hoping for a place on the roster in the next year or two. Most of them had improved their skills just by listening to Steve Kennedy.

Kennedy skated his players through a few drills, and then called for a scrimmage. Max, Sammy Fox and Kelly Jackson took their places on the first line, squaring off against Ollie Oliver, Peewee Halloran and Clarence Clarington-Clarke, who moved in for the faceoff. Cassidy and Leblanc played defence behind Max and his linemates. Marty Mitchell was in goal.

Riddell sulked on the bench, sitting well away from the high-schoolers. And he totally ignored Elmo Swift, the rookie from the Indian reserve.

"Let His Lordship have the puck," Leblanc whispered to Max. "We want to see what kind of stuff he's made of."

The puck was dropped, and Clarence scooped it up. It took only a few seconds for Max to see that he could skate. *Those figure skating sessions were a good idea,* he thought, as Clarence dashed in on the defence.

What a reception he got! Cassidy and Leblanc stepped into Clarence with reckless abandon. They gave him their elbows, knees and hips. Splattered him all over the ice and left him gasping for breath in a quivering heap of arms and legs. There was no sympathy shown from the bench.

"Hey, Clarence, did you get the number of that truck?" someone shouted.

Kennedy didn't say anything. The check was clearly illegal, and in a game Cassidy or Leblanc, or perhaps both, would have been sent to the penalty box—possibly for the rest of their careers. But Kennedy wanted to see how Clarence would react.

Groggily, the rookie staggered to his feet. He advanced on Cassidy, and the defenceman braced himself, waiting for the Brit to throw a punch in anger. Instead, Clarence gasped, "Sorry, old chap, didn't mean to run into you. Are you all perfectly all right?"

Cassidy and Leblanc gaped at each other.

"Did you hear the guy?" Cassidy grunted. "We smear him all over the ice and he says he's sorry!"

Leblanc took Cassidy by one hand. "Are you perfectly all right, old chap?" he asked, mocking Clarence.

"I'm tip-top, old boy," Cassidy replied. "But my bloomin' elbow is a little sore. That rookie chap ran right into it with his nose."

"Pity," said Leblanc.

Clarence went back to his position. Max felt sorry for the big guy and left him alone. But Sammy knocked him down with a clean check and Kelly Jackson gave him a ride along the boards that had him hanging onto the rail.

Leblanc caught him in the corner and nailed him into the boards with a crash that the mill workers on the evening shift must have heard a mile down the road—over the roar of the band saws.

Kennedy waited for Clarence to get mad—to pile into Leblanc and show him he wouldn't take any more dirty stuff. After all, his only chance to earn respect was to mop up the ice with at least one of his tormenters.

Once again, Clarence responded with a "Splendid check, old boy. Jolly good show. Sorry it was me who caught it."

Leblanc burst out laughing. He poked Clarence in the chest in what looked like a friendly way. But he added a little more zest to the punch at the last second and knocked Clarence on his backside.

"Sorry, old chap," Leblanc mimicked the newcomer. "Sorry it was me who threw it." He and Cassidy touched gloves again and roared with laughter.

Once again, Clarence skated away, smiling vaguely.

"Guess he's yellow, too," said Leblanc.

"Yellow as a ripe lemon," snorted Cassidy.

Cassidy and Leblanc were rugged young hockey players. They were determined to run Clarence off the team if they could, for the simple reason that they didn't think he was good enough to play at their level.

Neither did the newcomer's linemates, Ollie Oliver and Peewee Halloran.

Clarence led a rush and passed to Oliver. When Oliver was about to be checked he skimmed a return pass to Clarence. But the puck was several inches ahead of the rookie's outstretched stick. Moments later, another pass from Oliver to Clarence was about six inches behind him. When he reached back for it, he had to look down, and absorbed another stunning bodycheck. Then Halloran fired a pass at Clarence, who had to duck to avoid being struck in the head.

"Blimey!" he muttered. "I'm not playing very well."

Kennedy knew perfectly well what was happening. *The boys are telling him to go back to England,* he thought.

"Lay off of that stuff," he roared at the two wingers. "Give the guy a chance."

"Not my fault if the guy can't take a pass," mumbled Oliver.

After half an hour, Clarence's line had not scored a goal and had seen five scored against them, with Max accounting for three.

Clarence had absorbed enough bodychecks to last the average player a full season. Not once did he complain to Kennedy that he had become a target for every player he faced. On the other hand, not once did he dish out a bodycheck of his own.

Kennedy blew his whistle and called for a five-minute break. He took Clarence aside for a little chat.

"Why don't you lay into those guys, dish out some punishment of your own?" he asked.

Clarence looked at him in surprise.

"I'll admit they're a little rougher than I'm accustomed to," he said. "But really, old man, would it be quite the thing to do? Not cricket and all that."

"We're not playing cricket tonight," Kennedy told Clarence.

"Yes, sir, I know that. But my pater...my father that is, and my coach at school both stressed sportsmanship and the science of the game. They abhorred violence of any kind."

"Abhorred? That means they didn't like it?" Kennedy asked.

"Yes, sir."

"That coach of yours? Did he ever play hockey?"

"No, sir. He was too much of a pacifist for that. He was our mathematics master. He worked out plays for me on the blackboard. Had some interesting theories on how the game should be played."

Kennedy didn't know whether to laugh or cry. Finally he said, "Clarence, theories are all right, but a stick across the ankles or an elbow to the ribs is a fact in hockey. And the fact is, you'll be smacked around forever if you don't forget the theories and battle back."

"I'll give it some thought, old chap," Clarence said.

At the end of the scrimmage, Clarence had a black eye, a split lip and a collection of nasty bruises. Before leaving the dressing room in his fancy clothes, he said to his sour-faced teammates, "So long, you gents. See you tomorrow. Ta-ta for now." He gave them a friendly wave and disappeared into the night.

"Ta-ta, Clarence," bellowed Leblanc.

"Cheerio, old chap," said Cassidy. "Have a luverly evening. Tallyho and pip pip."

When Clarence was out of sight, they fell into each other laughing.

CHAPTER 4

OPENING NIGHT

The Indian River high-school band played martial music at the far end of the rink. A few of the young musicians even hit the proper notes. The lobby was jammed with hockey fans who bought programs and hot dogs and hot coffee before finding their seats in the stands for the opening game of the season.

Behind the Indian River bench, Coach Steve Kennedy stared moodily at the ice, his chin almost resting on his chest.

His team was about to open the season against the Hartley Wolverines, old rivals in the five team Northern League. Kennedy did not feel good about his team's prospects. The Wolverines were considered shoo-ins for the league championship.

Even so, Kennedy would have been more optimistic about an opening-night victory had it not been for his second forward line. The trio would simply not do. He had cajoled and threatened the wingers on the line to work with their new centreman, Clarence, but it had all been in vain. It was obvious that most of the Indians—except for the Mitchell brothers—resented the Englishman's presence. Of course, Kennedy resented him, too, but he knew that linemates had to work together no matter what.

As team captain, Max had privately pleaded with his teammates. "His skating is a big plus," he'd told them. "If we work with the guy, he may improve the rest of his game."

"Easy for you to say, Max," Oliver had grumbled. "You don't have to play with Clarence. He's just not a hockey player."

"And he never will be," added Leblanc. "He's a pantywaist, a sissy who won't fight back."

Kennedy knew most of the Wolverines by reputation. They were fast and experienced. In the first two minutes of the game, playing against Max Mitchell's line, they showed it. They slammed the puck into the Indians' zone from the opening faceoff and kept it there for most of the first shift. Marty Mitchell was called upon to make four difficult saves before there was a whistle.

Then came the moment Steve Kennedy dreaded. He relieved his starting line and sent out a threesome of Clarence, Ollie Oliver and Peewee Halloran.

"Let's hope their antagonism toward Clarence

will be forgotten under game conditions," he muttered.

But on the very first rush into the Wolverines' end of the rink, with Clarence positioned perfectly in the slot, Oliver refused to send him a pass. Oliver tried to take the puck around a defenceman and lost it along the boards. Moments later, Clarence broke up a play and slapped the puck over to Peewee Halloran, who bobbled it. Clarence had broken up ice, looking for a return pass. Instead, he looked back to find the Wolverines with the puck, streaking into the Indians' zone. Willie Wheeler, the visitors' top player, banged in a rebound from the edge of the crease, and the Wolverines took a 1–0 lead. Seconds later, Wheeler almost made it 2–0 when he took a hard shot from just inside the blue line. Marty stopped the rubber with his stick and whipped the puck up ice to Clarence. Clarence snapped it up, wheeled—and wham! He was blindsided by Lindsay, the Wolverines' 200-pound winger. Clarence wound up skidding along the ice on his backside, stopping only when he crashed into the boards.

He rose to one knee and saw Lindsay towering over him—ready for anything.

"Sorry, old boy," gasped Clarence.

Kennedy howled in frustration, yanked the line and sent his first-stringers back out.

The first-line forwards were accustomed to more than a few seconds respite on the bench. They knew why their coach was making a fast change— Clarence was a softy. Everyone could see it, except perhaps Mrs. Gray, who occupied a rinkside seat. When Clarence skated to the bench, she rushed over and patted him on the back, saying, "There now, Clarence, don't be discouraged. Perhaps you'd like an ice cream bar? Or a soda pop?"

"No, thank you, Auntie," Clarence murmured as he tried to ignore the laughter of his teammates. He hung his head in embarrassment.

Max was beginning to get angry. From the face-off he drew the puck back to Leblanc, then darted forward. Leblanc drilled a hard pass to Max in full flight. Before the Wolverines could react, Max leaped between the two defencemen and flashed in on goal. Porky Prentice, the Hartley goalie, saw Max wind up for a shot and braced himself. But Max was faking. He deked around Prentice and slipped the puck into the open corner of the net. Game tied.

The hometown fans bellowed their approval. Mrs. Gray clapped her hands and tossed her program in the air.

But Coach Kennedy couldn't leave his first-stringers out there too long. A minute later, he switched lines and Clarence replaced Max at centre.

Then came disaster.

The Wolverines began to concentrate on Clarence. They saw that he was the Indians' major weakness. Once, twice, three times they barrelled into him, trying to provoke him, and Clarence failed to retaliate. He took their punishment and didn't so much as utter a threatening comment or gesture in reply. With his wings ignoring him, two quick Hartley goals resulted.

The period ended with a glum-looking Steve Kennedy leading his charges back to their dressing room. It was a dismal start to a fresh season and he wasn't quite sure what to say to his players. It was obvious that some of them had no confidence in Clarence—they weren't about to feed him the puck.

Max couldn't recall ever having been in a dressing room so silent. Marty looked over at him and shrugged. He was stung by the three goals he'd allowed. He wondered how many more pucks he'd be scooping from his net in the two periods yet to be played.

Clarence stared down at the floor. Blood oozed from a cut over his eye. When someone knocked on the dressing room door, signalling two minutes to the start of the next period, he shook his head and began tightening his laces.

Kennedy stepped in beside Max as the team filed out of the room. "Get ready for plenty of ice time," he growled.

Early in the second period, the Indians' coach was delighted with the play of his first-stringers. Max scored his second goal of the game in the first minute of play, and he set Sammy Fox up for a breakaway two minutes later. Suddenly, the score was tied!

But the first line had been on the ice far too long, and they were dragging when they finally came to the bench. Mrs. Gray shouted, "Nice goal, Max! Nice goal, Sammy!" But the two forwards, their heads down, were too weary to even nod at her words of approval.

Steve Kennedy found himself thinking: *Mrs. Gray is a sweet old lady. And I'm glad she pays the bills. But I wish her seat was on the other side of the rink.*

The second line skated out. Once again, Clarence was checked to a standstill. Momentum swung to the visitors and they poured in on Marty Mitchell. He made a dozen saves, and some of them were spectacular. Then a shot bounced off a defenceman's leg and squirted into the net behind him—just over the line. Another bounced in off a goalpost, and a third goal was scored off a rebound.

As the period dragged on, the Wolverines grew stronger and the Indians sagged. The visitors began to pull away.

When the period ended, the visitors led 6–3. The

Indian River fans were crestfallen. Their team was taking a licking—a bad one. They suffered in silence, and made quite a contrast to the Hartley fans who'd bussed to the game—they rejoiced.

The third period was all Hartley. Max and his linemates tried to battle back. Midway through the period, Max connected for his hat trick on rubbery legs, but it was the last goal the Indians would score. Willie Wheeler knocked Clarence to the ice with a vicious check—no penalty—and raced in on Marty to score.

Three more goals were scored against Clarence and his linemates, two of them on the power play after the Indians—totally frustrated—began to take needless penalties. When the final bell ran, the Wolverines celebrated a 10–4 victory. By then many of the fans had filed sadly out of the rink. As a season opener, it was the most lopsided loss in recent memory.

Kennedy was shaken by the debacle. "Taylor is not going to be happy about this," he muttered. "A couple of more lickings and I'll be out of a job."

In the dressing room, the players dressed sullenly and hurried out into the night. Some had to be up early for the morning shift at the mill. Others had school to attend.

Kennedy didn't say much. Normally he would go around the room, complimenting players for the smart moves they'd made, gently pointing out to others the need to improve certain areas of their game. On this night, he remained silent.

He noticed that Clarence took a long time to get into his street clothes. Finally, he was alone with the coach.

"I say, Mr. Kennedy," he began politely, "if it won't disrupt your plans, I think you had better try someone else at the centre ice position. Frankly, I don't think I care to go on with it."

Kennedy was shocked. Clarence was quitting? He had not expected this, but new hope surged up within him. Without Clarence hindering his club, the Indians might have a future after all.

"Clarence, what's the problem?" he asked.

"To be honest, the hockey on this side of the pond is a little bit more strenuous than I'm accustomed to," he began. "I was hoping to fit in, Mr. Kennedy, but it's quite obvious I'm not wanted. Don't worry, I won't tell my aunt that the players resent me. I plan to move farther north of here—to Thunder Valley—and learn all about the lumber business."

"Well, this is a surprise," Kennedy stammered. "I was hoping you would fit in, too," he said honestly. Then he added, "You're a wonderful skater, Clarence."

Clarence beamed. "Yes, I am," he said. "Thank you. But there's more to hockey than skating. There's fighting, which I prefer to avoid. And I'll tell you why. In England I was on the boxing team at school. I didn't realize my punches were so strong. I hurt an opponent one day—hurt him badly."

"How badly?" Kennedy asked.

"He was hospitalized with a concussion. Luckily, he recovered. But he never competed in the sport again. He was my roommate."

"So the reason you don't fight back in hockey..."

"Is because I don't want to injure an opponent. Take my hand, Mr. Kennedy."

They shook hands. Steve Kennedy was amazed at the power in Clarence's grip.

"I'm much stronger than I look." Clarence tapped his head with a finger. "And I'm strong mentally, too. That's why I can ignore people who think I'm a silly Englishman who dresses and talks funny. Someday I'll probably run the mill for my aunt. And it will be because I've learned the business, top to bottom."

Kennedy was impressed. He saw a whole new side to Clarence in those few moments.

He said, "I'm sure you will, young man. I'm sure you will."

Clarence threw his skates over his shoulder and stopped at the door. He said, "Mr. Kennedy, you're a good man and a fine coach. But as much as I love hockey, I can't stay where I'm not wanted." He held out his hand again. "Thank you, sir. Tell the boys I wish them all the luck in the world."

CHAPTER 5

FINDING A NEW CENTRE

Max and Marty and their teenage friend Trudy Reeves had just ordered chocolate sundaes at Merry Mabel's. "A little ice cream will help take away the taste of defeat," Marty said to Max.

Before Max could reply, Sammy Fox burst through the door. He raced over and blurted out, "Did you hear? Did you hear the news?"

"What news?" Max asked.

"Clarence is gone! He quit the team, right after the game tonight. The boys are thrilled. It means we'll have a real second line again. We won't be pounded by the other three clubs in the league."

"That's surprising news, all right," Max said. "I kinda felt sorry for Clarence. Sure he was different, but he was a decent guy. He really didn't get much chance to show his stuff."

"Maybe he didn't have much stuff," Marty said. "He sure talked funny—pip pip, old chaps, tallyho and all those sayings. He was a fish out of water. And I can't figure why he let himself be knocked around on the ice. If you play like a chicken, you're bound to get de-feathered."

"Or get your throat cut," Sammy said.

Sammy was one of two players on the team from the nearby Indian reserve at Tumbling Waters. He and Elmo Fox came in from the reserve several miles to the north, to attend high school and play hockey. Sammy had become a star player playing alongside Max, and last season they had paced the Indians to the junior championship. Elmo, an orphaned youngster who excelled at lacrosse, had since joined the club and was making rapid improvement.

Having shared his news, Sammy turned to Trudy and said, "Hi, Trudy, what have you been up to?"

"I've been playing hockey, too. For the girl's team at high school."

"Really? You any good?" Sammy asked bluntly.

"My dad thinks so. He started teaching me to play when I was little. Backyard rinks and all that. I guess he wanted a boy, not a girl. Then I played on a boy's team for a year or two. At school, if we get a dozen people to our games, it's a mob. But I love the game."

"Trudy wants Marty and me to come to her game tomorrow after school," Max told Sammy. "It's on the outdoor ice behind the gym."

"I always go to watch Max and Marty play for

the Indians," Trudy said. "It's only fair they come to watch me."

"Brrr. Too cold out there for me," Sammy said.

"If you do come to my game, you have to promise not to laugh," Trudy said, wiping a dab of chocolate from her nose with a napkin.

Marty was puzzled. "Why would we laugh?"

"You might laugh at our goalie," she answered. "You'll see. But promise not to—you may hurt her feelings."

"Sure, we promise," Max said. "I'm afraid we've already hurt a hockey player's feelings today," he added, referring to Clarence.

On the following afternoon, Max and Marty trudged through the snow to the outdoor rink behind the school gymnasium.

"I heard through the grapevine that Trudy's the best player on the school team," Max said.

"Well, it's a pretty small school," Marty joked. "Remember, we promised her we wouldn't laugh. Wonder what that's all about."

"Something about the goalie," Max said. "Well, here we are."

The teams were skating out on the ice—the Indian River High girls in blue, the Hartley girls in red. Trudy and her teammates took warm-up shots at an empty net.

"Where's their goalie?" Max wondered.

"I think she's coming out now," Marty said, pointing at the open gym door.

Through the door, escorted by several teammates, the Indian River High goaltender made her appearance.

"Wow! It's Molly Bright," Marty gasped. "The biggest girl in school. She must weigh 300 pounds. I didn't know she could play goal."

By then, Trudy had skated over. She heard Marty's last comment.

"Molly can't play hockey," she explained. "Not really. She can't even skate. So we help her get dressed. Oversized goal pads. A baby's mattress roped around her waist because we couldn't find a belly pad to fit her. And we slide her across the ice into the goal. She holds onto both posts and tries not to fall down. She's had a dozen shutouts in the last two years. And won a school letter."

"Amazing," Max said, stifling a laugh.

"I get it," said Marty. "She shuts 'em out because there's no room to beat her. She fills every portion of the net."

"What's that weird thing on her head?" Max asked, staring in disbelief.

"It's an old water bucket," Trudy explained. "Molly was afraid of getting hit by a puck. So the school janitor found a bucket, punched some eyeholes in it and glued some sponge in the bottom. Presto! A hockey helmet extraordinaire. Molly wears it over a ski mask."

"And the handle of the bucket fits under her fat—I mean her chin," Marty observed.

Marty and Max couldn't help it—they burst out laughing. Molly looked ridiculous wearing a bucket on her head. They had never seen such a sight.

Trudy skated away, wagging her finger at them. "You promised," she said. "No laughing."

But the Mitchell brothers couldn't help but laugh.

Then the game began, and midway through the first shift, the boys no longer were chuckling. Their attention had turned to Trudy, and they were astonished at her skill on skates.

"She moves like a guy," Max said. "She's got all the skills: skating, stickhandling..."

"And shooting," Marty added. "Coach Kennedy calls them the three Ss."

"Look out, Trudy!" Max shouted in alarm. A huge player on the Hartley team cruised across the ice and threw a crushing bodycheck at Trudy. But crushing only if it had landed.

Trudy glanced up, saw the check coming and stepped into her rival. Pow! The big girl flew in the air and landed with a thump. A crack in the ice surface opened up at the point where she fell.

"Trudy just levelled that girl," Marty said admiringly. "Most guys don't hit that hard."

Max and Marty had met Trudy during the previous summer at the harness races. Trudy was a driver, a good one. Trudy and the Mitchells shared ownership of Wizard the Wonder Horse, a trotter that amazed the world of harness racing by capturing the 1936 Hambletonian. Max and Marty had no idea that, in addition to her harness-racing exploits and the fact she played on the basketball team and sprinted on the track team, Trudy was also a high-school hockey star.

She played a dazzling game that cold afternoon, leading Indian River High to a 13–0 victory over Hartley.

"Trudy scored ten of her team's goals," Marty said. "She's terrific."

"You're right, brother. If our junior team can't beat Hartley, at least our girl's team can."

"Let's wait for Trudy after the game and take her to Merry Mabel's for a victory treat," Max said. "Then we'll go home and mark this date on the calendar."

"Calendar? Date? What are you talking about, Max?"

"I'm talking about the hole we have at centre ice—now that Clarence has gone. This is the date we filled it."

"I still don't understand."

"It's so obvious, Marty. We found Sammy Fox and Elmo Swift, didn't we? Now we're going to be three times lucky. We're going to get Trudy to play for the Indians."

CHAPTER 6

A REPLACEMENT FOR CLARENCE

"I don't care how good you say she is," Steve Kennedy said to Max. "She can't play for the Indians." Max had called the coach and arranged to meet him in his office at the mill.

"But why not, Coach? I think she's as good as most of the players in our league. Better than some. Why not give her a tryout? See for yourself."

"I don't want her getting hurt. She'll be bumping into some pretty tough customers."

"And I say she can look after herself. You'll be surprised."

"Does she wear those white figure skates? With picks in the front?"

Max snorted. "Of course not. Some of the high-school girls do, but not Trudy. She's too smart for that."

"I'll bet she'll stop the game to fix her lipstick or powder her nose."

Max chuckled at the image. "Coach, you've got to be kidding. She'd never do that."

51

"Aw, I dunno, Max. What about crying? Does she cry when she's hit? Or misses a goal?"

"Come on, Coach, be serious. Trudy's a player. I've never seen her cry. She fell out of her tree-house once and she didn't cry—she was mad. She used some language that's not in the dictionary."

Then Max said the words that changed Steve Kennedy's mind.

"Coach, think of what a gate attraction she'll be. If she's good enough to play for us, fans will flock to the games. They'll think you're a genius. Women will love you for advancing women's hockey." Max paused, and then added, "Especially Mrs. Gray."

"Ah, yes, Mrs. Gray," the coach said, nodding his head. "Well, all right. Bring Trudy to practice tonight. But I'm still skeptical. Personally, I don't think women belong on a hockey rink."

"Coach, it's 1936. Women are into everything. If a war comes along in the next few years, I guarantee you they'll be in the armed forces. And more will be working on assembly lines, making bombs and bullets.

"Trudy's ahead of her time—like my mom was. Mom was a star with the Snowflakes a few years ago. Helped her team win the Lady Stanley Cup. Someday thousands of women will be playing hockey. Perhaps a few might even make it to pro hockey."

Coach Kennedy chuckled. "I doubt that, Max. Although I did read about a women's team in Preston, Ontario, with an impressive record."

"Right, the Preston Rivulettes. Won about 300 games and lost only a couple. Men's teams won't play them—they don't want to be embarrassed when they lose."

"Okay, okay," the coach said. "I said you could bring Trudy to practice, didn't I?"

Coach Kennedy was a little late getting to the team practice that night. Some accounting problems at the mill had kept him back. When he got to the rink, his players were already on the ice.

He looked for Trudy. When Max skated by, Kennedy called him over. "What's the matter, did your friend change her mind?"

Mac looked puzzled. "What do you mean, Coach?"

Kennedy said, "Where's Trudy? She chicken out?"

Max laughed. He pointed at a player skating circles around the rink, long hair flying behind her. "There she is. Out-skating most of us. Guess you didn't see her because she's just a blur."

"Very funny, Max. But gosh, she does skate well, doesn't she?"

"Come on, Coach. Throw your skates on. I think I've just found you another gem."

Kennedy had to admit it was true. Trudy Reeves exceeded his wildest expectations. She was a natural. She could skate, shoot, pass and score. And the male players brought out the best in her. They whooped when she skimmed a hard pass to the blade of their sticks and hollered when she took a return pass and drilled a shot into the corner of the net.

"Who needs Clarence?" Leblanc bellowed. "We've got Trudy."

Kennedy felt a lot better about the future when he watched his team at practice that night. With Clarence gone, the morale of the team improved. And the second line clicked smartly.

"Things are looking up," he told Max.

"We're anxious to wipe out that disgraceful performance in our home opener," Max told the coach.

Kennedy called for a scrimmage and tried Trudy at various positions—even defence. She handled the puck well, showed plenty of confidence and did not look the slightest bit out of place. But Kennedy was still not totally convinced.

"I promised Hack Riddell he'd play on the second line again," he told Max. "And Oliver's happy to be back at centre. We've got a game in Chatsworth on Saturday, but I'm leaving Trudy behind. She needs to get into top shape if she wants to play in this league. She won't find anyone mincing along in white figure skates in the Northern League."

The Chatsworth squad, like the Hartley Wolverines, was a power in the league. Their three imports—Bower, Smith and Dupont—had just missed catching on with the Boston Bruins minor-league affiliate.

The game was played at lightning speed, with both goalies striving for shutouts. Late in the third period, Max came from behind the Chatsworth net and slipped the puck between the goalie's skates. His goal silenced the Chatsworth crowd. Moments later, Max broke in with Sammy—two on one—and flipped a well-timed pass through the defenceman's legs. Sammy one-timed it to the upper corner. The Indians won 2–0 and the players mobbed Marty after the final bell.

At school the next day, Marty was the centre of attention. Everybody wanted to know about the game in Chatsworth and his shutout. Marty told a whopper to a couple of young girls.

"I got the shutout, but Max was the real star," he told them. "But he goofed badly on one play."

"What did he do?" they asked.

"Max was awarded a penalty shot. But instead of shooting the puck, he passed it."

Everyone howled at Marty's joke. But when Max came loping down the hallway moments later, one of his young fans asked innocently, "Did you really pass the puck on a penalty shot, Max?"

"What penalty shot?" Max began. Then he spotted Marty and his pals. He chased them down the hall and into their classroom.

The Indians' next game was on home ice—a mid-week encounter against the league's weakest team, the Carfax Cardinals.

"I've watched Trudy closely in two practice sessions," Coach Kennedy told Max on the morning prior to the game.

"And?"

"You were right. She's a player. She's earned a chance. She's our new second-line centre."

"Oh, boy," Max said. "Oliver loses his spot at centre and Riddell is going back with the scrubs."

Kennedy shrugged. "That's hockey," he said. "And if any of my players gives Trudy a rough time, he'll be warming his butt on the bench."

Max and Marty were well aware of the importance of the press. They phoned their father at the *Indian River Review* and gave him the news. On the following day his story appeared:

Female High-School Star to Play for Indians Against Carfax Tonight

Coach Steve Kennedy stunned not only the Northern League but also hockey fans in general when he announced today that the Indians would introduce Trudy Reeves, a 16-year-old high school phenom, to top-flight junior hockey. Reeves will suit up against the Carfax club in her debut, playing centre on the Indians' second line. Clarence Clarington-Clarke, a player from England, who retired from the game this week and left town, formerly occupied the position.

The signing of Reeves has created much talk among local hockey fans and around the league. Area fans are expected to jam every corner of the arena for the game against Carfax. Reeves admitted she was "nervous" but "hoped to do well." She said she was grateful to her friend, team captain Max Mitchell, for recommending her, and to Coach Kennedy for giving her a chance to play.

Not everyone endorses the move. It's reported that two of the imports on the Indians are upset, possibly because they will get less ice time if Reeves can do the job.

"It's a great day for women's hockey," said Trudy's father, Michael Reeves, who taught her to play the game. "Too bad they don't have an Olympic team for women players. I'm sure Trudy would be on it."

The signing of Trudy created great excitement in Indian River. As predicted, it brought an enthusiastic response from Mrs. Gray.

She phoned Steve Kennedy and told him he was a genius.

"A brilliant idea, Steve," she praised him. "I wish I had thought of it. That Max Mitchell is one smart boy. You know, I have a niece living in the Boston area and she plays hockey. I was thinking…"

Oh, no! thought Steve. *She's got another relative she wants on the team.*

Mrs. Gray continued. "I was thinking you might get Trudy to send my niece a little note. My niece is only seven, and she's thinking of giving up hockey for ballet lessons…"

"I get it, Mrs. Gray," Steve replied, relief in his voice. "I'm sure Trudy will be glad to do that. And we'll send your niece a hockey puck signed by Trudy."

There was all the atmosphere of a playoff game when the Indians faced the Carfax Cardinals at the arena that night. During the warm-up, a dozen high-school girls shouted "Trudy! Trudy! Trudy!" as she skated around taking her warm-up shots.

But Coach Kennedy wasn't about to start his second line. He took Trudy aside and told her,

"Only a fool tests the depth of the water with both feet. So keep your head up! Be ready for anything. And make the first shift a short one."

The Cardinals had a first-rate starting lineup, but their reserves were weak. Max and his linemates did a fine job of checking their counterparts for the first two minutes. Then there was a whistle, and Trudy Reeves got the nod from Coach Kennedy. She slipped over the boards and skated into the faceoff circle. The noise was deafening. Oldtimers in the crowd couldn't remember when any player had received such an ovation—just for skating on the ice.

"Trudy! Trudy! Trudy!"

On the bench, Max grinned and turned to Sammy. "Isn't it great? Listen to them!"

"I just hope all that noise doesn't rattle her," Sammy said.

In the faceoff circle, the opposing centre, Butch Brownlee, smiled at Trudy and said something to her. The crowd assumed he was being a good sport and wishing her well. Instead, through his fake smile, he was saying, "Make me look bad, sweetie, and I'll chop your legs off. I'm warnin' you."

Trudy snapped back, "I won't make you look bad. You can't look any uglier than you do right now."

The puck was dropped and Trudy scooped it back to her defenceman—Leblanc. She dashed away with Brownlee in pursuit.

The Indians worked the puck into the Carfax zone, and Trudy took a pass from Peewee Halloran and slapped the puck at the Carfax netminder. He wasn't expecting a female player to raise the puck, and it almost flew past him, grazing the crossbar.

The fans responded with a mixture of cheers and groans.

If Trudy was nervous she didn't show it, and moments later she gave her supporters what they were waiting for—a goal.

Brownlee was skating laboriously into the Indians zone. Trudy was backchecking and moved in behind him. Suddenly she called out, "Butch! Butch!" She slapped the blade of her stick on the ice.

Thinking the voice was a teammate, and without looking back, Brownlee dropped the puck behind him. He turned to see it smack against Trudy's stick. She wheeled and raced away in the other direction, the Carfax players scrambling to catch up. Trudy moved in alone, deked the goalie—and scored! She circled the net, arms upraised, when suddenly she skidded to a stop. A furious Brownlee, skating full tilt, charged at her and tried to nail her to the boards. Wham! Trudy's quick stop saved her from a vicious bodycheck, and Brownlee smashed into the boards shoulder first. He fell to the ice gasping.

"Five minutes!" shouted the referee, leaning over Brownlee. "Deliberate attempt to injure." Then he added, "You big jerk!" When Brownlee staggered to his feet and skated to the penalty box, several of the Indians followed. They challenged him to turn and fight, defending their new player. Leblanc called him "a yellow dog."

Meanwhile there was bedlam! The celebration lasted for five minutes. The fans were ecstatic. They had come to see Trudy score and she had not disappointed them. And on her first shift!

Wisely, Coach Kennedy changed lines, and Trudy received a lot of back-thumping and glove-touching from her teammates when she reached the bench. The only two who looked on with disinterest were Hack Riddell and Ollie Oliver.

Max was so excited he yelled, "Attaboy, Trudy! I mean, attagirl, Trudy!"

The rest of the Indians appeared to get a lift from Trudy's opening goal and Brownlee's angry charge. They went on to humiliate the Carfax squad by an 8–2 score. Max connected for three of the goals and set up Sammy Fox and Kelly Jackson for two more. Trudy had three assists in the second period.

Hack Riddell wasn't on the ice very long, and helped kill off a couple of penalties.

After the game, Coach Kennedy breathed a sigh of relief. He told the sports editor of the *Review*:

"I've got to admit I was nervous. It was a big gamble, putting a 16-year-old female player in against those mutts from Carfax. Brownlee threatened to maim her but I heard Leblanc give him an earful. 'You lay a finger on Trudy Reeves and I'll open you up and peek inside. Then I'll tear your heart out.'" Steve Kennedy laughed. "You know, hockey players are always yapping at each other, making threats. None of them ever amount to much. But when Brownlee heard Leblanc say that, I'm sure he thought he was serious. And maybe he was."

Max and Marty were planning to stop in at Merry Mabel's on their way home. Trudy would have joined them, but her parents were driving her straight home.

Marty was a slow dresser and Max waited patiently at the door. The other players filed out until only Marty, Elmo Swift, Ollie Oliver and Hack Riddell remained.

Coach Kennedy passed Max and said, "Great game tonight, kid. See you tomorrow."

"You want to join us for ice cream, Elmo?" Max asked. Elmo, a quiet young man, lived in a boarding house near the arena during the school year. "No, thank you," he said politely. "I've got homework to do."

"How about you two?" Max said to Oliver and Riddell. It was another attempt on his part to make friends with the city boys, even though they made it clear they preferred to keep to themselves.

"Another time, maybe," Oliver said.

"Okay, see you then," Max said, as Marty followed him out the door.

Max had borrowed the family car and he was halfway to Merry Mabel's when he pulled to a stop.

"What is it?" said Marty.

"I left my library book at the rink," Max said. "I need it for a test I have in school tomorrow. We'll have to go back."

A few minutes later, Max parked near the front door of the deserted rink.

"It sure looks different with the crowd gone and the lights out," Marty said.

"I was afraid the night watchman might have locked up by now," Max said, "but the front door's still open."

They walked down the corridor and were approaching the dressing room when Max put a hand on Marty's shoulder. "Listen!"

"Sounds like somebody moaning," Marty whispered. "Maybe an animal got in our dressing room."

"Or a thief," Max said quietly. "Let's find out."

The brothers shoved open the door and were shocked by what they saw.

Elmo Swift was flat on his back on one of the

benches. His shirt was torn and his hands and feet were taped together with hockey tape. An old red and white hockey stocking was stuffed in his mouth.

While Hack Riddell was holding Elmo down, Ollie Oliver was beginning to shave the hair on his head.

Max was outraged. "What's going on?" he bellowed, racing over to shoulder Riddell off the bench and onto the floor. He lashed out at Oliver and knocked the razor from his hand. Marty joined in and shoved Oliver on his back.

"Take it easy, boys. Take it easy." Oliver said, flashing a smile. "It's just an initiation. It's an old tradition in hockey."

"Yeah, we just realized Elmo's a rookie," Riddell said. "Rookies always get shaved."

"Not on this team!" Max shouted, still furious. He yanked the stocking from Elmo's mouth, stripped away the tape that bound him and helped him to his feet.

"You okay, Elmo?"

"I'm okay," the Indian youth answered. His face was pale and his hands were shaking. He glared at his two tormentors. "They call it an initiation. I say they picked on me because they don't like Indians."

"Aw, we were just having a little fun," Oliver said. "No need to get upset."

"Yeah, we initiated six kids on our team in Boston last year. Shaved them bald. As I say, it's a tradition."

"And I say it's barbaric," Max replied. "I suppose you would have gone after Trudy next."

"I admit we were thinking of it," Riddell said. "She'd look a lot different bald. More like a hockey player."

"You know she'd quit the team in a minute if you did that," Marty exploded. "And her folks would probably sue the club."

"Get out of here!" Max shouted, his hands folding into fists. "You boys are sick."

"Sure, Max, sure," Oliver said. "We made a mistake. It was all in fun—we didn't know... Say, you're not going to tell Coach Kennedy, are you? He might kick us off the team."

"No promises," Max yelled. "Just get out. Go home."

"Sorry, Elmo," Riddell said, as he and Oliver scrambled out the door.

CHAPTER 7

MORE TROUBLE FROM THE IMPORTS

The real test for the Indians came a few nights later, when they journeyed by bus to Hartley for a return game with the Wolverines. All of the players were up for the game, eager to avenge the disastrous defeat in the season opener.

Max had decided not to tell Steve Kennedy about the initiation of Elmo Swift. Not yet. Max was anything but a tattle tale, and Elmo himself was willing to let bygones be bygones.

"Look, Max," he said, taking off his cap. "Since I lost some hair anyway, I shaved my head on both sides and now there's a wide strip down the middle. Some great warriors have worn their hair like this. And the girls at school think I'm cute."

It was difficult to win a game in the Hartley arena at any time. The ice was rough and the lighting was poor. The crowd was unruly and tended to throw programs, popcorn and other items at the opposing players. During the first period, one fan threw a box of chocolates at Marty Mitchell, and there was a delay while the sweepers came out to clear the chocolates from Marty's goal crease—but not before Marty scooted out and sampled a couple, nodding his head in approval and drawing a laugh.

Fortified by the sweets, Marty played a stellar game, allowing just two goals—both by Willie Wheeler.

Kelly Jackson and Max scored goals early in the third period to silence the Hartley fans and tie the score. Trudy Reeves didn't score, but she set up three good chances and the crowd gave her a big round of applause when she came off the ice at the end of her shift.

Kennedy formed a new line of Riddell and Oliver—with Elmo on left wing—and was pleasantly surprised at the results.

"If Coach Kennedy had known those two guys tried to shave Elmo, he might not have put the three of them together," Max told Marty during the second intermission.

"Those two dorks wouldn't even make room on the bench for Elmo to sit next to them," Marty snorted. "They ignore him off the ice, even though Elmo set them up with some really good passes. Did you notice they don't even talk to him in the dressing room."

Thanks to Elmo's playmaking, Oliver and Riddell each scored a goal in the final minute of play, much to the chagrin of the Hartley fans. Now the debris they threw on the ice was aimed at the hometown players. Oliver and Riddell seemed happy for once with the amount of ice time they got—and talked at length about the pair of goals they'd scored to help win the game.

Marty nudged Max in the dressing room. "If those two guys had backchecked like they should," he complained, "Wheeler would never have scored. I would have had a shutout."

"I was thinking the same thing," Max replied. "They don't put much effort into their checking, do they? They leave that to Elmo."

"Oliver told me it was humiliating to be replaced at centre—first by a no-talent Englishman and then by a silly girl," Marty declared. "He said he'd be leading the team in scoring if Kennedy had handled him properly."

Max rolled his eyes. "It's too bad," he said. "Oliver and Riddell could really help us. I mean, look at how well Cassidy's worked out. But their attitude...well, they just don't get it."

Coach Kennedy said he was pleased with the 4–2 victory. The bus ride back to Indian River was a pleasant one and the players were home and in bed shortly after midnight.

Kennedy hadn't seen anything of Clarence since the night he turned in his uniform. He had expected to be called on the carpet by Mrs. Gray and lectured for not keeping Clarence on the team. But evidently Clarence hadn't complained to his aunt. The next time the coach saw Mrs. Gray—in the lobby of the arena prior to a game—she was surprisingly agreeable. He noted that she was wearing a new winter coat—grey in colour—with hat and gloves to match.

"I'm so happy you're having some success with the hockey team," she cooed. "Before he left, Clarence told me you were a very good coach—and a very nice man. And my niece thanks you for the puck. She wants to come visit, to see Trudy play."

"It was nothing," said Steve. "And Clarence? Is he doing well?"

"Wonderfully well. He's a supervisor already—at the mill in Thunder Valley. It's about an hour's drive from here."

"Is he playing any hockey?"

"Some—just to stay in shape. He mentioned a small league he plays in." She laughed. "It's called the Bakery League."

"The Bakery League?"

"Yes. A baker in town bought the jerseys for the players, so the boys named their teams after his baked goods. There's the Butter Tarts and the Apple Squares and the Gingerbread Men. Clarence plays for the Cream Puffs."

"Clarence is a Cream Puff?" the coach said. He almost added, "How fitting!" but decided against it.

"He said the other players get quite rough with him," Mrs. Gray said earnestly. "So he's changed his style of play, whatever that may mean."

"Give him my regards," Steve said, tipping his fedora. He walked away chuckling. The Cream Puffs indeed. He thought of what Riddell had said about Clarence when he played for the Indians. "They should call his line the Doughnut Line," he had quipped. "No centre."

As the season wore on, the Indians, with more harmony in the dressing room, won more games than they lost. At the halfway mark in the schedule, the Indians found themselves in a race for first place with the Hartley Wolverines. Max, Sammy and Kelly were among the top ten scorers, and Marty's goals-against average was exceptional. He seldom allowed more than three goals per game. Oliver and Riddell were inconsistent, playing well when they felt like it and poorly when they didn't. But they managed to chip in a few goals, and Kennedy, in an effort to be supportive, was quick to congratulate them for their efforts.

It was a big mistake.

"Glad you appreciate us, Coach. We think we're playing better than the first line," Oliver said. "Max Mitchell isn't all that good."

"What do you mean?" Kennedy barked. "Mitchell's the best centre in the league."

"Maybe so, but we think we're better two-way players," Riddell bragged. "And we think we're the reason the crowds have been so good. And that means a lot of money in gate receipts."

Kennedy almost gagged when the two imports told him they believed they were better two-way players than Max. He was suspicious. "What are you two getting at?" he asked.

"We think we should be rewarded with a little bonus," Oliver said bluntly. "You're not going to win the title without us. Anyone can see that."

"They can, can they?" Kennedy responded. "Well, maybe it's time I got a seeing eye dog. How much do you greedy boys have in mind?"

"We figure 500 dollars would do it—500 apiece, that is. It's not much when you consider all that extra money from the gate."

"Most of that money goes to support hockey in this community," Kennedy countered. "Our equipment, our travel costs. The minor league in town would fold without the funds we provide."

Oliver and Riddell shrugged. "That's got nothing to do with us," Riddell said.

"Why not take it up with Mr. Taylor," Oliver suggested. "He signed us. He likes us. So does old lady Gray."

"I'll do that," Kennedy said. "But don't get your

hopes up. And that's Mrs. Gray to you hotshots."

He went to Taylor's office at the mill and told him of the players' demands.

To Kennedy's surprise, Taylor seemed to think Oliver and Riddell deserved some compensation. What he didn't tell the coach was that he had made a deal with the two imports on the day he signed them.

He had told Oliver and Riddell at the time, "Somewhere along the way I'll try to get you boys some money—despite what Mrs. Gray says. But if I do, you'll have to turn back 20 percent to me. Call it a fee for services rendered."

Oliver grinned. Mr. Taylor had just indicated he was as devious as they were. "That's okay with us," Oliver said. "We know about kickbacks."

"But not a word of this to anyone," Taylor had cautioned them. "I could lose my job."

Now Taylor was caught in an awkward situation. Oliver and Riddell had asked the coach for some cash, and Kennedy was plainly angry about their demands. The two players should have come to him.

"Those arrogant pups," Steve Kennedy said. "Trying to hold us up for money under the table."

Taylor sighed and pretended to be deep in thought. Finally he said, "Well, I suppose we'll have to pay them. We're in a real bind. The additional gate money will take care of it. And we want that championship."

Kennedy shook his head vigorously. He was surprised at Taylor's stance.

"If you pay them, they'll be back again for more. And more after that. And if the other players find out about it, they'll expect similar treatment. It isn't fair to them."

It hadn't been a hard decision for Kennedy to make. He had learned right from wrong at his mother's knee. He couldn't understand why some people—like Taylor—had difficulty making moral judgments. And why others—like Oliver and Riddell—tried to cheat or use blackmail to get what they wanted.

He was prepared to resign if the manager allowed himself to be exploited by a couple of greedy teenagers.

Finally, Taylor came to a decision. He would go along with the coach. Later, he told himself, he'd find a way to pacify the two imports.

He said, "By gosh, you're right, Steve. Good thinking. I like a man with principles. I have all kinds of principles myself. I pride myself on being honest and trustworthy."

Sure you do, Kennedy thought. *About as honest and trustworthy as a burglar.*

"Stall the two imports if you can," Taylor urged. "But we won't pay them a red cent. Don't kick them off the team, though, whatever you do. I promised them they'd play."

Oliver and Riddell weren't stupid. When Steve Kennedy told them the club was taking their request "under advisement," they nodded knowingly. Kennedy was stalling.

In their next game, against the Summit Sailors, the two played listlessly in the first period.

Kennedy took them aside and barked at them, "Come on, you two. Get the lead out! If you don't, I'll trade you to the last place Summits."

Riddell smiled. "You can't do that, Coach," he said insolently. "Mr. Taylor has to approve any trades. And he gave us no-trade contracts. Didn't you know?"

Steve Kennedy growled and turned away. No, he hadn't known.

In the second period, Oliver and Riddell apparently tried a little harder. They managed to break up enemy attacks, but when they got within scoring range themselves, something always went wrong. Either a pass would go astray or a shot would fly wide of the net.

The Sailors, sensing that they were up against a weakened team, swarmed in looking for an upset. They beat Marty for a pair of goals.

Toward the end of the period, Oliver skated through the entire Sailor team—just to show he could do it if he cared. But then he pulled the goalie and missed the open net.

He skated past the Indian bench and said to Kennedy, "I would have had it, Coach. I just need a little incentive." Then he pulled off his glove and rubbed his fingers together.

The message was clear. But Kennedy remained firm.

"Nothing doing," he barked, his face red with anger.

It was one of those nights when the home team—the Sailors—got all the breaks. In the third period, a puck deflected off Cassidy's rear end and slipped between Marty's pads. Another was kicked into his net, and the referee, a local man, allowed the goal.

Max played about 40 minutes with Sailors draped all over him. Even so, he broke loose for a pair of goals. And with two minutes to play, Trudy scored from a sharp angle.

The Indians trailed by a goal.

Steve Kennedy watched the big clock at one end of the rink. With a minute left to play, he called for a timeout and waved Marty to the bench.

He turned to Max. "I know you're tired, Max, but I can't rely on either of those two loafers, Oliver and Riddell. I want you to be the extra attacker."

"Don't worry, Coach. I want to be out there for the final minute."

The Sailors skimmed the puck out of their zone

and down the ice. Max raced back for it and wheeled at his own blue line. He dodged one checker, then another. The puck stayed glued to his stick. Kelly Jackson called for a pass and Max threaded the puck between the legs of a defenceman and onto Kelly's stick. Fifteen seconds to play!

Jackson bowled over a Sailor who tried to cross-check him into the end boards. He saw Max flying into the slot and whipped the puck out to him. Max one-timed it high and hard into the net. Bull's eye! The red light flashed. Tie game! Ten seconds to play.

The Indian bench erupted. Sticks slapped the boards. Max and Kelly grinned at each other and slapped gloves. Teammates moved in to hug them.

"Now we'll beat them in overtime," Max whooped. "They're all finished—so tired they can hardly stand up."

From the faceoff, the final ten seconds clicked off the clock.

Overtime!

But no!

Max watched in disbelief as the referee picked up the puck and started to leave the ice. The Sailors skated off and disappeared, heading for their dressing room. The fans made their way to the exits.

Max chased after the referee. "Hey, Ref, there's overtime," he shouted. "Where are you going?"

"No, there's no overtime," the referee said. "It's late and I want to go home. Each team gets a point."

"But you can't..." Max stammered. "It's a rule. There's overtime. We may need that extra point to win the title."

The referee turned nasty. "You got wax in your ears, kid? I said there's no overtime. Not tonight. Besides, two of your players said it was fine with them."

The official clumped off down the corridor.

"Wait!" Max called out. "I'm the captain. What about the coach? Who said it was okay to end the game? Who said we'd settle for a tie?"

The referee turned and shouted over his shoulder. "Your two prima donnas—Oliver and Riddell." He entered the referee's room and slammed the door.

The Indians had no choice but to leave the ice.

Max relayed the shocking news to Coach Kennedy, who glared at Oliver and Riddell when they stepped through the gate. "Nice game, you two," he said derisively.

"Thanks, Coach, we tried our best," Oliver said flippantly. "And we got a tie. Nothin' wrong with that."

The long bus ride home was not a pleasant one.

"This is not good," Kennedy mumbled to himself. "Not good at all. We can't possibly win the title with those two bozos in the lineup."

CHAPTER 8

LOOKING FOR SYMPATHY

The following morning, Steve Kennedy drove slowly through the streets of Indian River. He was deep in thought, agonizing over the sluggish play and mercenary attitude of the two imports, Oliver and Riddell. He had to do something about the situation—but what?

Finally, he turned his car in the direction of the mill, parked in front of the main door, strode inside and barged into Mr. Taylor's office. "I want to get rid of Oliver and Riddell," he said bluntly. "Even if it leaves us short of players and costs us the title."

Taylor was shocked and upset. He rose from his chair and took Steve by the arm.

"Please don't do that, Steve," he pleaded. "I promised them they'd be regulars. Perhaps I over-rated them, but..." Taylor hesitated, and then leaned closer to the coach. "Besides, Mrs. Gray has taken a personal interest in them. She wants them to succeed."

Kennedy's eyebrows shot up. "Mrs. Gray? What does she have to do with this?"

Taylor crossed the room and closed the office door. He paced back and forth before saying, "Coach, Oliver and Riddell met with Mrs. Gray a few days ago. They had her in tears. They told her they'd both had difficult childhoods, that they'd never had toys at Christmas, never had birthday parties, that their folks had threatened to place them in a home for wayward juveniles. They confessed that they'd stolen some money as kids and bullied the other kids in town. But now with the Indians they had a fresh chance to make something of themselves by playing hockey and holding down good jobs."

"Oh, boy," sighed Kennedy. "I didn't know any of this..."

"They were afraid to tell you. They figured you only liked kids with solid backgrounds—like the Mitchell brothers. They told Mrs. Gray they were afraid you were going to find a way to get rid of them, despite the no-trade contracts I gave them."

"I guess I had decided to do that," Kennedy said. "And what did Mrs. Gray tell them?"

"You know what a softy she is, Steve. She was moved to tears and hugged them. I was there, and I shed a few tears myself."

I'll bet you did, Kennedy thought. He couldn't imagine Taylor with tears in his eyes—unless someone held an onion under his nose. "Then what happened?" he asked.

Taylor shrugged. "Well, she felt so sorry for them that she gave them a few dollars each. She told them she couldn't interfere with your coaching decisions. She did it once—with Clarence—and realized it was a mistake. She said she would try to help them as much as possible. Today she baked them a big cake, and she's having them over for dinner tomorrow. Oliver told her it's his birthday."

"Next thing you know she'll be adopting them," Steve muttered, not really listening. "If I were her I'd keep my jewellery locked up when they're around."

"Steve, that's unfair," Taylor grumped. "I'm surprised at you."

"I know, I know, but I can't help it. I don't trust those two. They never mentioned an unhappy childhood to me. But I suppose I may be wrong about them. Let me think about it."

In his car, Kennedy thought perhaps he'd been a little unfair to Oliver and Riddell. Maybe he should have been less stern as a coach and more fatherly in his treatment of them. He might have been more forgiving of their insolence and conceit if he'd known they'd been mistreated as kids. Perhaps he could give them a second chance, spend more time with them, counsel them and be a good role model for them. He'd pass along some of his favourite proverbs, like "Think classy, and you'll be classy," "Unless you're the lead dog, your view never changes" and "If you want to lead the band, you've got to turn your back on the crowd."

On his way to the arena, Kennedy heard his stomach rumble. He decided to stop at Merry Mabel's for a sandwich and a cup of coffee. On the counter he picked up a copy of the local paper. While he was reading the sports page, something crossed his mind. He frowned, thinking of his earlier conversation with Mr. Taylor. Taylor had said something about Oliver celebrating his birthday tomorrow—at Mrs. Gray's house. "I'll be right back, Mabel," he called out.

He ran out to his car and reached for the briefcase he'd left on the back seat. He went back inside, regained his seat and leafed through some papers in the briefcase.

"Ah, here they are," he said aloud. "The forms my players signed when they joined the Indians. And here's Oliver's." He glanced at the birth date on the card and roared, "Why, that little liar! Mabel, his birth date is in August, long after the season is over!"

Mabel had been talking to a customer and hadn't heard every word.

She turned to him and cupped an ear. "What's that, Coach? You want a date with me? In

August? After the season is over?" She laughed. "That's long-range planning, isn't it? And say, did you just call someone in here a liar?"

"No, no, no, Mabel, I never...well, two of my players can't be trusted. They're looking for sympathy and possibly money—from someone we all know and respect."

"I'm sorry," Mabel said, expertly sliding a ketchup bottle along the counter to a waiting customer. "You were mumbling, Coach. Were you talking to me?"

"No, Mabel, I'm talking to myself," he sighed. "Being a coach will do that to you."

Just then, Tom Cassidy, his third import, entered the restaurant. He called out a greeting to Mabel and ordered a cola and a slice of her famous apple pie. He sat on the stool next to his coach.

"Hi, Coach, reading the obituaries? Your name in there?"

"No, Tom, not today. But the league standings are. With a little luck we can still win the title."

Kennedy liked Cassidy. He was an intelligent player who fit in. A good team man.

"Say, Tom," he asked. "You played in the city league last year, right? That's where Mr. Taylor scouted you."

"That's right, Coach."

"Did you know Oliver and Riddell very well?"

"No, not well. They played for another team."

"Know anything about their backgrounds, their family life? Were they underprivileged kids? Were they from broken homes?"

Cassidy smiled. "Heck, no, Coach. Quite the opposite. They're upper-middle-class kids. Spoiled rotten by their folks. They're only here in Indian River because their folks got fed up with their antics and kicked them out. There was some trouble with the law. Petty theft, I believe. Some bullying at school. I heard they shaved the hair off some kids. Their folks told them to get out and grow up—to make something of themselves. I thought Mr. Taylor would have told you all about them."

"He didn't tell me enough, obviously," the coach replied. "Thanks, Tom. By the way, you're a real asset to the hockey club."

Cassidy beamed. "And it's a pleasure to be coached by one of the best in the business," he replied. "Say, are you finished with the sports page?"

Steve sipped from his coffee cup. His thoughts returned to Oliver and Riddell. Perhaps he could tolerate them for few weeks, but they wouldn't be back next season. And he reminded himself to warn Mrs. Gray about them. She was such a sweetie, but she was gullible, ready to listen to any kind of sob story. He would remind her to be on her guard. And to keep her purse out of sight.

He sighed and sipped his coffee.

He decided he had much to be thankful for despite his problems with Oliver and Riddell. Max was playing the best hockey of his life and Marty was much more solid in goal than he'd expected him to be. And then there was Trudy...

He chuckled out loud, thinking of Trudy. Tom Cassidy glanced over for a moment, shrugged and returned to the sports page.

The big surprise was Trudy. She didn't score many goals, but her checking was tenacious. And her playmaking was second only to Max's. She was cool under pressure, and once opponents discovered bodychecks or other mean-spirited tactics couldn't rattle her, they treated her as they would any other player. In each rink around the league, a separate dressing room was set aside for her. And in each rink, a large group of young women formed a cheering section for her. They waited patiently for her outside her dressing room door and she signed autographs willingly—up until she had to run to catch the team bus back to Indian River.

Kennedy's face brightened whenever he discussed Trudy with his captain.

"You found us a gem, Max," he said into his coffee cup.

Midway through the season, Trudy had been

approached by the manager of the Preston Rivulettes, the best women's team ever assembled. "Come and play with us, Trudy," they had asked her. "Our team is famous. We never lose a game. You'll play in the national championships every year."

"No, thank you," she replied. "I'm flattered but I made a commitment to Coach Kennedy and the Indians. They discovered me, and I wouldn't dream of deserting them now. Besides, I'm having too much fun to think of playing anywhere else."

Coach Kennedy appreciated her loyalty. The season had been a real eye-opener for Trudy. He wondered what she thought of some of the bizarre incidents along the way.

Kennedy recalled a night in Chatsworth when the temperature dropped to 30 below. Fans who came to the rink in cars left their engines running in the parking lot. They didn't want to come out after the game only to discover that their cars were frozen and wouldn't start.

That was the night he had kept six players on the ice and the rest in the dressing room, gathered around the pot-bellied stove. When it came time for a change of lines, he had a fan knock on the door, and the substitute players came rushing out, their heads covered with toques and earmuffs.

Another night, in Hartley, the refereeing was pitiful. The arbiter's name was Blinker—Ben

Blinker. Late in the game, during a line change, a fan slipped out on the ice carrying a paper bag. He went nose-to-nose with the referee and cried, "Blinker, you're a stinker!"

The referee said, "Oh, yeah? Well I think I smell pretty good."

The fan bellowed, "You won't after this!" He pulled his pet skunk from the bag and pushed it into the arms of the ref. The official fell back, dropped the pet and headed for the exit, followed by the skunk. Only after he was assured that the skunk had been taken away did he consent to return. From then on he was known as "Stinker" Blinker.

Playing at home one night, Max banged skate blades with an opposing player when he rushed in on goal. Seconds later he lost his balance and fell. After the game, he met Mrs. Gray in the lobby and she asked him about his tumble.

Max shrugged. "I lost an edge, Mrs. Gray. It happens sometimes."

She took his arm. "An edge, you say. Well, let's you and I go right back on the ice and look for it."

Coach Kennedy chuckled out loud and Mabel gave him a look. "You all right, Coach? Is it the coffee?"

"No, Mabel, I'm just thinking."

Kennedy recalled another night, when Marty was hobbled by a bruised ankle before a game and couldn't play. It was Trudy who suggested using big Molly Bright as a backup. Max and Marty convinced him to give Molly a try. The hometown crowd roared and applauded when Molly appeared and promptly got stuck in the gate leading onto the ice. She finally bulled her way through the gate but stumbled and collapsed in a heap on the ice. The crowd thought it was hilarious. There was more applause and a few whistles. The bucket Molly wore as a helmet fell off and bounced across the ice surface and while Trudy retrieved it, the rest of the players collectively heaved Molly onto a toboggan and hauled her to the goal crease. They propped her up, plunked the bucket over her head and patted her broad back. The Indians went on to play a marvellous defensive game, allowing only a half dozen shots on goal. Only one of them gave Molly trouble. An opposing forward fired a shot that hit Molly in the belly. She doubled up as he raced in for the rebound. But Molly was falling forward, and when she toppled over, her full weight squashed the forward in his tracks. He screamed as he was buried under 300 pounds of flabby female. Only his quivering legs could be seen. Players from both teams rushed to his aid. The Indians hauled Molly upright while the Sailors pulled their terrified teammate to safety. The Indians beat the Sailors 4–0.

"Ha ha ha!" laughed Kennedy.

Heads turned in the restaurant. Cassidy put down his newspaper and gave the coach a puzzled look. Mabel rolled her eyes.

What the coach didn't know was that after the game, Molly Bright spoke with Max and Marty.

"That game did wonders for my self esteem," she said. "Thank you for endorsing me. And your mother has been a real inspiration. She's got me on a weight-loss program. Just wait until next year—I'm determined to lose at least 100 pounds. Nobody will laugh at me again. Thanks, guys!" A tear spilled from Molly's eye as she gave them both a bear hug, all but lifting them off their feet and squeezing the breath out of them with her powerful arms. Her embrace caused Marty to fart loudly.

Molly's goaltending gave Marty an idea. When he was ready to play again, he showed up for a game with his baseball catcher's mask and wore it against the Carfax Cardinals. The Carfax fans and players hooted in derision. "Halloween's over!" one fan bellowed. Marty didn't care. The mask saved him from at least one nasty cut. No one was laughing when he skated off with a shutout.

"Are you going to keep wearing the mask?" Max asked him after the game.

"I may—after some adjustments," Marty answered. "The straps are a bit loose. And it was hard to see the puck at my feet. But a goal mask is definitely in my future. I don't know why all goalies don't use them."

"Neither do I," Max said. "Maybe all the players should wear more facial and head protection."

"See the good ideas I come up with," Marty bragged. "Someday you'll be proud to call me a genius."

"Genius? You're a goalie, Marty. And a catcher in baseball. Guys fire balls and pucks at you at 90 miles an hour. They barrel into your crease and spike you sliding into home plate. And you chose those positions. Some genius!"

Coach Kennedy chuckled aloud at the memory of Marty chasing his brother around the dressing room.

Mabel took his empty coffee cup away. "I think you've had enough, Coach," she said. "My coffee seems to be making you giddy."

CHAPTER 9

DESERTING A WINNING TEAM

Every game the Indians played drew a packed house. When the schedule reached the three-quarter mark, it became clear that the league title would go either to the Indians or to the Hartley Wolverines. The winner would earn home-ice advantage in the playoffs and be favoured to move on to the national championships, played on artificial ice in Montreal.

The crucial game of the regular season was a match in Hartley involving the two front-runners. If the Wolverines won they would hold a three-point lead in the standings. A victory by Indian River, however, would narrow the margin to a single point. And the Indians had five games left to play, while the Wolverines had four.

Kennedy was an anxious man as he prepared to send his team out for the opening whistle against Hartley. But in his heart he knew that his team was good enough to defeat the local club. The Indians had overcome many obstacles in their quest for the championship, and with the Mitchell brothers leading the way, their chances of a trip to Montreal looked good.

Max agreed. "I know we can beat these guys," he said to the coach. "Marty's playing like an NHLer and Trudy's playmaking has been outstanding. The best thing is—we're all pulling together now. Nobody resents Trudy's presence—not like they did Clarence. It's true Oliver and Riddell griped about her at first, but lately not a peep, although they do ignore her most of the time."

"They've been surprisingly quiet," Kennedy said. "I'm trying to give them more ice time, although they're both weak checkers. I'm keeping my fingers crossed they don't create a problem with first place up for grabs. In the past they've been whiners and complainers—crybabies. But I think one of my proverbs shut them up."

"Which one was that?" Max asked.

Kennedy smiled. "I told them most players would rather be ruined by praise than saved by criticism."

Max grinned. "Did they get it, Coach?"

"It took a few minutes. But I think they did. By the way, I caught Oliver smoking."

"You did? How did you handle that?"

"I told him that a cigarette was a pinch of tobacco, wrapped in paper—fire at one end, fool at the other."

"I hope he got the message," Max said.

In the dressing room, the Indians appeared to have only one thing in mind—beating Hartley.

"Now go get 'em!" Kennedy barked. "Go out and wallop those Wolverines."

It was a fast, brilliant game, as every fan in the North Country expected it to be. The Hartley fans exploded in cheers when the Wolverines grabbed an early lead. Willie Wheeler, their slippery little centre, burst around Oliver, slipped between the Indians' defence and whipped a hard shot to the upper corner of Marty's net.

"Doggone it," Marty said to Max, "I shoulda had it. If that little runt comes down here again, I'll clobber him."

"Forget about him," Max told Marty. "We'll get that one back."

With a few seconds to play in the period, Max swooped in behind the Indians' goal, grabbed the loose puck and started up ice. He looked for a winger to pass to, but both were covered. So with a great burst of speed, he skated up the middle of the rink. Wheeler slid over and tried to check him, but Wheeler was a lightweight and Max elbowed him aside. The Wolverine defencemen were backing up, but too slowly. Max flew between them and dashed in on Porky Prentice, the Hartley goaltender. He spotted an opening—upper corner—and lashed a high shot, aiming for the hole.

But Prentice moved fast and got an arm up, and the puck rebounded off his elbow. Prentice fell to the ice as the puck skipped in front. Max corralled it with the blade of his stick—too late for a second shot. Instinctively, Max circled the net with the puck, ice chips flying from his flashing blades. He swooped back in front and tucked the puck in the far corner. The red light flashed just before the buzzer sounded to end the period.

It was a brilliant goal and the Hartley fans knew it. Many of them burst into spontaneous applause—appreciation for the skill of a visiting player. It didn't happen often in Hartley. Marty flew down the ice, hopping on his skates in joy. He caught up to his brother as the teams left the ice.

"Great goal, Max!" he yelped. "You said you'd get one back and you did!"

Max's goal gave the Indians a lift, and they peppered Prentice with shots in the second and third periods. But the Hartley netminder—diving, sprawling and leaping—blocked every puck and kept his team in the game.

At the other end of the rink, Marty Mitchell put on a similar show, robbing the Wolverines of at least six goals.

With a minute to play, the score remained 1–1. Then Prentice made a foolish mistake. He slashed at Max with his goal stick as Max flew through his crease. Max tumbled to the ice and slid heavily into the boards.

The referee hesitated, and then blew his whistle. Two minutes for slashing.

The Indians would have a man advantage for the final minute. Coach Kennedy sent out Trudy to replace Cassidy on the point. Cassidy had taken a hard shot to the ankle and was limping.

Max snared the puck from the faceoff and whipped it back to Trudy. She moved in a few feet, faked a shot on goal and threw the puck back to Max. He trapped it, and then heard Trudy cry out, "Max! Max!"

Trudy was flying in from the blue line, rapping her stick on the ice. Calmly, Max wristed a pass onto the tape of her stick. Trudy unleashed a rising shot that sailed over Prentice's shoulder and into the upper corner of the net. The red light flashed. Trudy leaped high in the air, arms raised, celebrating her goal.

The Hartley fans groaned, and then went silent.

The final few seconds ticked away, and the game was over.

The reception for the Indians when they arrived back in town on the team bus was tumultuous. Despite the late hour, a large crowd greeted the players.

"Good work, Coach," beamed John Taylor, shaking Kennedy firmly by the hand. "The league title is in the bag."

But years in hockey, perhaps the most uncertain of all team games, had left Kennedy fully aware of the folly of counting chickens before they were hatched. Or even after they were hatched.

"We still have a few games left to play," he told Taylor. "Nothing is certain in hockey."

"Nonsense," the mill executive retorted. "You'll make toast of the other chump teams in the league. And Max Mitchell is going to be the league MVP."

"Let's hope you're right," muttered Kennedy.

But something was bothering Kennedy, a premonition of trouble. He could feel it in his bones. A couple of times he surprised Oliver and Riddell in earnest discussion that ceased abruptly when he entered the room.

He had scheduled a light workout on the evening before the Indians were to leave town for their next game—against the Summit Sailors.

On his way to the arena, he stopped in at Merry Mabel's for his evening meal and was seated at the counter when Mabel told him he was wanted on the phone. It was Mrs. Gray and she sounded distraught. "Steve, I want you to send Oliver and Riddell to see me immediately. I'm very upset with them." She began to cry.

"Mrs. Gray, I'll go get them and bring them to your house. Can you tell me what's wrong?"

"Not on the phone. Just bring them here."

The line went dead.

Steve Kennedy reached for his coat and was about to leave when the phone rang again.

"Another call for you, Coach," Mabel said.

He didn't recognize the voice.

"Coach, it don't matter who's calling but I think you oughta know a couple of your players are about to beat it outta town."

Kennedy was shocked. "What do you mean? Who is this?"

The caller ignored the question. "I live in the same boarding house as Ollie Oliver and Hack Riddell. They checked out today. Took all their belongings down to the station. They're taking the evening train to the city. And they skipped out on their rent."

The caller was left talking into the mouthpiece. Kennedy dropped the receiver and snatched up his hat and coat. He plunged out of the restaurant and into the night, leaving the door swinging behind him.

Oliver and Riddell were nicely settled in their seats on the train. Riddell looked at his pocket watch.

"Two more minutes and we'll be leaving this burg forever," he muttered. They had been too spineless to tell Kennedy face to face that they were deserting the team.

"Going for a little trip, boys?"

They looked up, startled, shame-faced and guilty. Steve Kennedy was standing in the aisle, looming over them.

The deserters glanced at each other. Then Oliver said, "We left a note for you at the boarding house, Coach. Something came up at the last minute."

"So you're leaving the team for good."

"Yep." The young men nodded.

"We got an offer from the Ravens," Oliver said. "A team closer to home. The manager said we'd be on his first line. Not like here. And he promised me I'll be captain."

"And I'll be assistant captain," Riddell added. "The Ravens need leadership."

"Some leaders you two are," muttered Kennedy, looking at them grimly. "The Ravens, huh? An outlaw team in a bush league. Just the place for you quitters. You realize this is a pretty rotten trick you're playing on me. Not to mention Mrs. Gray, who's treated you like her own sons."

They shifted uneasily. "The Ravens are in the playoffs," Riddell said. "The deadline for signing players is tomorrow."

"Are they paying you?"

Oliver squirmed. "Yeah, they are. A couple of hundred each. That's more than you were willing to cough up."

"And we won't have to play with girls," Riddell said.

Oliver cleared his throat. He said, "Besides, there was trouble at the mill. Somebody stole some money from the payroll office—1,000 dollars. We didn't want to get blamed for something we didn't do."

"We're no thieves," Riddell said indignantly.

A bell clanged. The train lurched and inched forward.

"Go to blazes, both of you," Kennedy snarled over his shoulder as he hurried back down the aisle and leaped down to the platform.

The train was soon out of sight around a bend in the track.

Steve Kennedy decided to drive over to Mrs. Gray's house. Somebody had to tell her she'd never see Oliver or Riddell again.

Back on the train, the two deserters grinned at each other and slapped hands.

Oliver looked around. No one was watching them. He pulled a wad of money from his pocket—mostly 50-dollar bills. He flipped through it.

"Is it all there?" Riddell asked.

"It sure is. A thousand bucks—500 apiece. It was nice of Mr. Taylor to leave it right where we could find it."

"He said he would get us some cash. And he did—even if he had to steal it. That cheapskate

98

Kennedy would never have paid us."

Oliver snorted. "Taylor thought it would buy us for the rest of the season. He'll be furious when he finds out we skipped town with the money he stole."

Riddell reached into his pocket. "When we hock these little items we'll have at least 2,000 bucks," he chortled.

Oliver was surprised. "What have you got there?"

"Some jewellery. A couple of diamond rings."

"You devil. Where'd you get them?"

"From a silly old woman, dear old Mrs. Gray. At your so-called birthday party, I had to go to the bathroom, remember? Well, I went to her bedroom, too. And I found these little baubles in her jewel box."

"Good job, Hack. And another good reason for leaving this hick town. When she finds out they're missing, she won't think we're her little angels anymore."

"Who cares what the old dame thinks?" Riddell chortled.

Hours later, Oliver and Riddell climbed off the train in the big city and stretched their arms and legs.

Riddell flashed a devilish smile. "Who said crime doesn't pay?" he asked.

"Whoever said it doesn't know squat," answered his pal.

They started across the street carrying their gear. Before they got to the other side, Riddell grabbed Oliver by the arm.

"You better give me my 500 bucks now," he said.

"Don't be impatient," Oliver answered sharply. "You'll get your share."

He held up the rings. "Look at them sparkle," he said. "They're real diamonds, all right."

Just then a taxi pulled around the corner, travelling fast. His fare was late getting to the station. The driver spotted two men in the street and yanked on the wheel. His cab skidded on a patch of ice.

"Look out!" he screamed as his car veered toward the pedestrians.

Whack!

The fender of the cab caught Riddell in the knees, sending him flying. Oliver was smashed by the cab's grill and knocked back about 20 feet. A large number of 50-dollar bills flew in the air and sailed in all directions. Strangers chased after them and scooped them up. Most of them felt pity for the injured men and returned the money to a policeman who had rushed to the scene. Others pocketed the bills they gathered up and hurried off with them.

A man handed the policeman two diamond rings. "I found these next to the kid with the smashed leg," he said.

The policeman examined the rings. "Expensive ones," he said. "They could be stolen."

"And the money too?" the man asked.

"Sure. Why not?" the policeman said. "We'll get these kids to the hospital. After they're patched up we'll have a nice little talk with them at the police station."

A crowd gathered. A grey-haired man pushed his way through the crowd. "I'm a doctor," he said.

Moments later, he barked, "Better call an ambulance. One lad has a broken ankle, the other a broken wrist."

"Some skates fell out of their bags," a bystander noted. "They must be hockey players."

"Not any more," the doctor said. "At least not for the rest of this season."

CHAPTER 10
REPLACING TWO DESERTERS

Steve Kennedy left Mrs. Gray's house in a sour mood. He had never seen her so upset. She had told him that some of her most expensive jewellery was missing, and that she suspected Oliver and Riddell had made off with it.

"Now you tell me they skipped town," she said to Steve. She shook her head sadly. "We'll never see those two again. Or my rings."

"I should have warned you about them, Mrs. Gray. I meant to. Then things began to happen..."

"I'm not blaming you, Steve. It's just too bad those two couldn't have been more trustworthy— like the Mitchell brothers. And been more honest—like you. And Mr. Taylor."

Steve almost choked. He was about to say something about James Taylor, then thought better of it. He had no proof that Taylor couldn't be trusted. It was just a feeling.

By the time he reached the rink, Steve Kennedy had calmed down. He had lost two of his imports—but who needed such slackers? Still, they had to be replaced. But how?

"I should have kicked those two mutts off the team when they tried to force money out of us," he muttered. "Taylor persuaded me not to. And hockey talent is scarce. I doubt there's another Trudy Reeves in town."

Fortunately, the Indians' next game was against the Sailors—a weak club. It was a road game on the weekend. His Indians should win—even playing with a depleted lineup.

In the dressing room, his players were suiting up for practice. But there was a chill in the room. The Indians had heard about the desertions and they were upset and angry.

"Listen, team," Kennedy said. "A couple of deserters have crossed us up. They're gone and they're history. And good riddance to 'em. I'm going to borrow a couple of lads from the juvenile team in town. Remember, all we have to do right now is win that game on Saturday against the Sailors. And we're gonna do it. You fellows up for it?"

There was a mild cheer but it wasn't as hearty as Kennedy would have liked. He was thankful when Marty shouted, "We're gonna do it, Coach. Watch our smoke! We'll make those Sailors walk the plank."

Two kids from the juvenile team slipped into the dressing room, lugging their gear. Max went over and greeted them and introduced them around. They were excited about joining the Indians. Eager but shy.

On the ice, Dayton, the centreman, showed a nice turn of speed, but he was an awkward stick-handler and the wingers on his line soon began rolling their eyes at his errant passes. Stewart, the other kid, was no better. But the newcomers tried hard. They were wildly anxious to make good.

Following a scrimmage, Max stayed on the ice, working with Dayton. When he came in, Kennedy said, "What do you think?"

"He's a good kid," Max said honestly. "So is Stewart. But they're both a year or two away from playing at this level. Too bad we need them now. Or someone like them."

"What about a kid from a nearby town?" Kennedy asked. "We've got a 40-mile limit. Remember, that's how we got Sammy."

"It's pretty late to go scouting for fresh faces," Max countered. "And if there was an outstanding kid out there, we'd probably have heard about him. I'll call my Uncle Jake. He goes to a lot of games in the small towns north of here. And he knows his hockey."

"It's worth a try," the coach replied. "But it looks like we'll have to play the hand we've been dealt, and pray that Dayton and Stewart can help us out. We've got to have a third line."

Dayton and Stewart suited up for the game against the Sailors. But whenever Coach Kennedy sent them over the boards, their inexperience showed. Hoots and catcalls from the Summit fans rattled their nerves—they'd never played for so many spectators before—and they coughed up the puck frequently. The Sailors scored three goals against the rookies and won the game 3–2.

"You were right, Max," Kennedy sighed. "They're still a year away from this calibre of hockey. I'm sending them back to the juvenile team."

Max snapped his fingers. "Say, I just thought of someone else who might help us," Max said. "I don't know why I didn't think of it before."

"You did?" said Kennedy. "Who is it?"

"Promise not to laugh? It's a crazy idea."

"Promise."

"Charlie Chin."

"Max, you're kidding. Charlie can't play hockey. You know that. He's…he's…missing a hand!"

"I know," Max replied. "But I'm sure we can figure out a way for him to hold a hockey stick. A kind of sling or something. He's a great skater. We don't need him to score goals. We need someone to keep the other team's best players from scoring goals. Charlie could do that—if he could hold a stick."

"You're something, kid," Kennedy said with a smile. "And I do believe you're onto something. Now why didn't I think of that?" The coach jumped up. "Get Charlie in here. Talk to him. Try to figure out a way to make it work."

At first Charlie was overjoyed to think there might be a place for him on the Indians' roster. Then he said soberly, "But it would take some medical expert from the city to make a fancy fitting for my false hand. It might cost 1,000 dollars. My family can't afford that expense..."

Max said confidently, "Come with me, Charlie. I know a fellow here in town who might do it for free. He's a real hockey fan. And he's a marvel when it comes to working with leather."

"Who's that, Max?" Charlie asked as he followed Max out of the room.

"He's the man who owns the livery stable in town. When Trudy drove Wizard the Wonder Horse to victory in the Hambletonian, he made the harness for Wizard. His name is Albert Picard."

Max was right about Albert Picard being a marvel with leather. In less than an hour, he fashioned a deep pocket of leather that fit nicely over the butt of a hockey stick. He attached the pocket to Charlie's metal hand with thick rubber bands. The bands held the shaft of the stick in place but still allowed freedom of movement.

"That's incredible!" Charlie said excitedly when he tested the contraption, and he thanked Albert profusely.

"Let's go back to the rink," he urged Max. "I'll

bet I can even pass and shoot the puck with this thing on."

Coach Kennedy was in a despondent mood when he entered the arena before the Indians' next home game against Chatsworth.

In the lobby, he ran into Mr. Taylor, who made it clear he was unhappy with the progress of the club. He was particularly upset over the loss to the Sailors.

"You brought in two kids who were scared to death out there," he complained. "It cost us the game."

"So?" Kennedy had replied. "I gave them a chance. Sometimes young players rise to the occasion. Dayton's going to be a fine centreman someday. He's just not ready yet."

"I could have told you that," Taylor growled. "If we're desperate enough to try new faces, perhaps we should start behind the bench—not on it."

Kennedy exploded in anger. "Don't threaten me, Taylor," he hissed. "If you want to fire me—do it! Just remember, it's the imports you brought in who gave us the most trouble. They had some skills but not much character."

He turned and stormed off to the dressing room.

He closed the door behind him and turned to face his players. He blinked and his mouth fell open.

There on a bench, sitting next to the Mitchells,

was Clarence. And next to him, holding a hockey stick in some sort of leather apparatus, sat Charlie Chin. Both young men were grinning from ear to ear.

"Hiya, Coach!" bellowed the Englishman. "Surprise, surprise! It's great to see you again." He jumped up and pumped Kennedy's hand, forcing him to wince and almost buckling his knees.

This was not the Clarence Coach Kennedy remembered. He barely recognized him. Gone was the wispy moustache. The tan overcoat, the silk scarf, the brown shoes—gone. Even his accent was less pronounced.

Clarence wore a lumberman's jacket and work boots. His blond hair shot out in all directions from beneath a peaked cap.

"Clarence!" Kennedy gasped. "Is that you? You've...you've changed."

"I hope so, Coach. Maybe for the better. Living with the mill workers has toughened me up some. I hear you're a little short-handed. I thought you might consider taking me back. The Mitchell brothers thought it might be a good idea. But they said you're still the boss." He slapped Charlie on the shoulder. "My new pal Charlie thinks he can help out, too. I've already nicknamed him the Chinese Checker."

Kennedy looked over at Max and Marty. They nodded their heads. "Give Clarence another chance," the bobbing heads said. "And Charlie, too. What have we got to lose?"

What have I got to lose, Kennedy thought. *Aside from my job as coach.* But he wanted a little more information. He turned to Clarence.

"Mrs. Gray says you've been playing hockey this season. But in some funny league."

"Yes, sir. The Bakery League. I'm leading the Cream Puffs in scoring. We walloped the Lemon Tarts the other day 8–1. And we wiped out the Jelly Doughnuts 6–0 last week to take over first place. The Doughnuts have the best equipment in the league. I say it's because they have all the dough." He roared with laughter and all the players in the room laughed too. They got the joke.

"I even enjoy a fair scrap now and again," he added with a wink. "Although I still try not to hurt anyone."

"I can't believe this is the same guy who was here earlier in the year," Marty whispered to Max. "He's so confident. And funny."

"I called Uncle Jake the other day," Max replied. "He lives not too far from Thunder Valley. Uncle Jake went to see Clarence play a couple of games, and told me he was burning up the league."

"And Clarence just showed up here?" Marty asked. "He didn't even call the coach?"

"He tried to, Marty. But a blizzard up north knocked out the phone lines yesterday. He came down on the train."

"How about it, Coach?" Clarence said. "I feel like a new man. I won't let you down."

Kennedy's sour mood had changed. He began to laugh.

"All right, Clarence. If the fellows agree, I'll give you another chance."

Kennedy turned to Charlie Chin and placed a hand on his shoulder. "Charlie, I know Max and Marty think the world of you. You think you can play for me? You know, with this new whatchamacallit on your hand?"

"I can play," Charlie said confidently. "I may not score, but I'll check like crazy. You won't be sorry."

"That's good enough for me," said the coach.

There was a ripple of applause around the room. It may not have been unanimous, but it was approval enough.

Clarence had a final question. "I'm still eligible, aren't I, Coach?" he asked. "You didn't tear up my playing card and throw it away? I can hardly blame you if you did."

Coach Kennedy smiled. He reached deep into his coat pocket and pulled out a wrinkled card.

"It's got your name on it, Clarence," he said. "You're still a member of the team." He pulled out another card—a blank one. "And I've been saving one last card in case someone shows up at the last minute. I'm gonna fill it out Charlie 'Conacher' Chin."

"C'mon, boys," Clarence shouted when he was dressed in Oliver's discarded gear and had donned his old number—13. "Let's go pump in some goals!"

A buzz spread through the stands when the Indians—led by Clarence—skated out to host the Chatsworth club.

Clarence flew through the warm-up, chatting it up with his teammates and occasionally waving to the crowd. A large group of lumberjacks from the Bakery League had come down on the afternoon train, there to offer support.

"Clarence! Clarence! Clarence!" they howled. Clarence grinned and flipped a couple of pucks high into the crowd, souvenirs for a couple of his pals.

"Don't shoot too many pucks up there," Max cautioned Clarence. "Pucks cost the team 20 cents apiece."

It was Max who suggested that Clarence should start at centre, with Trudy on one wing and Elmo Swift on the other.

"He's raring to go, and we'll find out right away if he's the new Clarence or the old Clarence," Max told the coach. "And I don't mind centring the second line."

"Good idea," muttered Kennedy. "But don't get

your hopes too high."

There was a huge cheer from the lumberjacks when Clarence skated to centre ice for the opening faceoff.

"They might as well holler now," grunted Kennedy. "They may not have much to cheer about the rest of the night."

"Moose" Dupont, the Chatsworth centreman, all but licked his lips when he saw Clarence lining up against him.

I've heard of this guy, he said to himself. *The yellow Brit. A softy. A marshmallow on skates. Let's see how he reacts to this little trick.*

Before the puck was dropped, Dupont flicked his stick from the ice to just under Clarence's jaw, breaking the skin and drawing a trickle of blood.

"Oh, sorry," he said in mock remorse. "My mistake."

Clarence looked him straight in the eye. "It's all right, old chap," he said. He took off a glove, leaned in and placed his big fist against Dupont's nose. "But do it again and you'll have these knuckles to deal with."

Dupont swallowed, and then snorted in disbelief. *He's fakin'*, Dupont told himself. *He's yellow as a sick canary.*

The puck was dropped, and Dupont snapped it up. He threw it back to a defenceman, circled back and took a return pass. Legs pumping, he burst up the middle of the ice and—wham! Clarence surged from nowhere and stepped into him. It was a thunderous bodycheck, and Dupont's legs flew east and west as his body crashed to the ice. He lay there moaning while Clarence scooped up the loose puck and flew down the ice with it.

He barrelled through the defence, cracking one defenceman in the jaw with a shoulder check, and then swooped in on goal. His rising shot from 20 feet slammed into the goalie's chest, sending him to his knees. And when the rebound came out, Clarence snapped it up and flipped it over the goalie's head into the upper corner of the net.

The crowd went wild. First goal to the Indians in the first few seconds of play! The only player who missed seeing the red light flash was Dupont. He was on his hands and knees, crawling along the ice toward his bench.

Coach Kennedy was almost too stunned to cheer.

"Holy mackinaw!" he muttered. "Was that really Clarence? If it was, I hope he stays around this time."

Next to him, Max was banging the boards with his stick. "Way to go, Clarence!" he howled. "What a goal!"

Max turned to the coach. "Uncle Jake told me they toughened him up in the Bakery League. Players up there are Cream Puffs and Butter Tarts in name only. They kicked him around at first, but when he started kicking back, they soon got out of his way."

"Guess he was too much of a gentleman for those lumberjacks," the coach said. "They knocked all the gloss off of him."

"Not all, I hope," said Max. "A guy can be a hockey player and still have good manners."

Clarence's lightning-fast goal shocked the Chatsworth club, and before they could recover Max scored a goal and Trudy added another.

Then the Indians took two penalties in the span of 20 seconds.

"Get out there, Charlie. Let's see what you can do," the coach bellowed.

Charlie Chin pushed the butt of his stick deep into the leather pocket and leaped over the boards. Over the next two minutes he won the hearts of the hometown fans with a display of checking that was truly amazing.

He darted after Dupont, who tried to lead a rush, elbowing him off stride and knocking the puck back to the end boards. He drove in and pinned the puck to the boards with his skates, forcing a whistle and a faceoff deep in the Chatsworth zone.

Dupont tried another rush but Charlie caught up to him from behind, hooked the puck off his stick and slapped it back into the Chatsworth zone.

The crowd began to hoot and holler. One old-timer shouted in the ear of another, "I haven't seen penalty killing like that in 20 years. His skating reminds me of myself when I was young. What did you say they call that little guy?"

"The Chinese Checker," his pal replied. "And you never skated like that in your life, you old fart."

The visitors lost their poise and spent most of the evening trying to make Clarence pay for his devastating hit on Dupont. They slashed at him, elbowed him and threatened him verbally. Clarence laughed at them. One frustrated opponent even leaped on his back during a rush along the boards. Before the referee could signal a penalty, Clarence shook the player off and sent him flying into his own team's bench, where he sent several teammates sprawling.

The fans erupted in jeers and laughter.

The Indians won the game 5–0 and Clarence— with two third-period goals to complete a hat trick—was named the first star.

Well-wishers mobbed him when he left the ice. But not before he grabbed Charlie Chin by the seat of the pants and hoisted him onto one broad shoulder.

"Give him a cheer!" Clarence bellowed. "Let's hear it for the Chinese Checker!"

The roar of the crowd was deafening.

CHAPTER 11

PLAYOFF PRESSURE

Suddenly, with the addition of fresh faces, a dash of newfound enthusiasm and strength down the middle, the Indians were the hottest team in the North Country.

They surged to the top of the standings, passing Hartley and capturing the league title by a single point.

"Guess we won't need that overtime point we missed earlier, after all," Marty chortled. "Now we'll breeze through the playoffs and get to play in Montreal."

"Don't be too cocky," Max warned. "Anything can happen in hockey."

But Marty proved to be an accurate prognosticator—at least for the first round of the playoffs. The Indians polished off Chatsworth in three straight games in the semi-finals and swept the first three games of the final series against Hartley.

"Get ready for Montreal, fellows," Marty bellowed, after shutting out the Wolverines in two of the three wins.

"I told you, don't be cocky," Max cautioned. "We're still a win away from that trip. We've been good but we've also been lucky. And good luck doesn't last forever."

Max was right. Lady Luck was with the Wolverines in the next two games. Hartley squeezed out a 1–0 victory in game four on a shot that took a lucky bounce and fooled Marty. In game five, the Indians hit the goal posts three times without scoring and the Wolverines scored the game's only goal on a shot that bounced off Cassidy's skate, changed direction and eluded Marty's desperate grab.

Game six was a North Country barnburner that left both fans and players limp with exhaustion before it was over. Max and Willie Wheeler excelled with their playmaking and both set up two goals and scored two apiece. Marty and his counterpart, Porky Prentice, made several breathtaking saves, and Clarence pounded several Wolverines into the ice with devastating but clean bodychecks. At the end of regulation time, the score was tied 4–4.

Then in overtime, a play developed that will be long talked-about in North Country hockey circles. Willie Wheeler crashed into Marty's crease with the puck. Cassidy pushed him down and tried to whack the puck off Wheeler's stick. It bounced away and Cassidy stepped on it. Then Wheeler pulled on Cassidy's leg and he toppled over, falling heavily on top of the puck. He also fell on Wheeler's head.

The whistle blew, stopping play. The referee, pointing at Cassidy, barked, "Penalty shot!"

"What do you mean?" screamed Cassidy.

"You fell on the puck in the crease. That's a penalty shot. Don't give me an argument!"

He took the puck to centre ice. "Hey, Wheeler, take the penalty shot!" he shouted.

Wheeler, who was still groggy from the goal-mouth collision, eagerly jumped at the chance. But his head wasn't clear. He circled the ice and wound up. He zeroed in on the puck, took it on his stick and flashed toward the goal.

The fans screamed in sudden shock and surprise. Wheeler was streaking toward his own goal!

Porky Prentice, who'd been leaning on his goal net, had no stick. He'd placed it atop his net along with his gloves. He was hoping to witness Wheeler score the game winner—but at the other end of the rink.

Wheeler fired the puck from 20 feet and Prentice, gloveless and stickless, kicked it aside. No goal!

"What are you thinking?" Prentice screamed at Wheeler. "You went the wrong way, you idiot."

Only then did Wheeler realize the enormity of

his error. He looked up in the stands. Some fans were screaming at him in anger. Others were roaring with laughter. Wheeler was humiliated. He skated toward the referee. "What happens now?" he asked.

The referee could barely restrain himself. "You just committed the biggest blunder in hockey history!" he roared.

"Give me another chance," pleaded Wheeler. "You've got to. Otherwise, I'll never be able to live this down."

"He had his chance," bellowed Steve Kennedy through cupped hands at the bench. "He blew it."

The referee had to make a quick decision. He'd never seen a player take a penalty shot against his own team. He'd never heard of such a thing. Penalty-shot shooters, ever since the exciting play had been introduced, had always gone one way— toward the opposing goalie.

"You get another chance, Wheeler," he ruled. "You want a compass for this one?"

"Thanks, Ref," said Wheeler gratefully. Without wasting another second, he took the puck, raced in on Marty and rifled a shot to the upper corner of the net. Game over. The Wolverines won 5–4 and tied the series.

Despite giving up Wheeler's overtime goal, Marty was chipper on the bus ride back to Indian River.

"Aw, we'll wrap up this series on home ice tomorrow night," Marty grinned. "The Wolverines have been lucky to get this far. And the whole town will be out to support us."

Marty was right about the fan support. The arena walls bulged with the press of humanity, and the ovation the crowd gave the Indians prior to game seven could be heard in the next county. The noise became even louder when Max scored the first goal with a blast from the slot. Then Clarence split the Hartley defence to score a second goal with the first period not ten minutes old.

Molly Bright, the backup goalie, lurched to her feet to cheer Clarence. But she stumbled awkwardly, and her skate came down heavily on Cassidy's foot.

He howled in pain. "I think you broke my toe," he screamed and limped off to the dressing room.

"I'm so sorry," Molly said. She began to cry.

Minutes later, Max stepped on a gum wrapper a fan had thrown on the ice. He lost his balance and crashed into the end boards. He was carried off, bleeding from a cut over his left eye.

The loss of two key opponents gave the Wolverines a boost. Willie Wheeler slipped around his check and scored with a sharp angle shot on Marty.

With ten seconds left in the period, Wheeler was tripped up as he tried to crash through the

Indians' defence. He failed to score but he flew through the air and barrelled into Marty, who flipped over backwards in the net, straining his back muscles. Marty struggled to his feet and signalled to the referee that he was okay, and play resumed. The period ended with the Indians in front 2–1.

In the dressing room, everyone huddled around the Mitchells.

"First you, Max," Coach Kennedy said. "How seriously are you hurt?"

"The team doctor says I'll need some stitches," Max said. "And I feel a little groggy. But I can play."

"Make sure the doc says it's okay," Kennedy declared. "How about you, Marty? I can see you're in pain."

Marty sighed. "I pulled something in my back when Wheeler hit me. It's hard to straighten up. But I'll be okay in a few minutes."

"We can always put Molly Bright in goal," the coach suggested.

"Look at her, Coach." Marty snorted. "She stepped on Cassidy's foot. She feels rotten—so shook up she can't possibly play."

"Well, neither can Cassidy," was the rueful reply. "He may have a broken toe."

"I can play," Cassidy grunted. "I'll find out after the game if my toe is broken. I'm no quitter. Not like Oliver and Riddell."

With Marty struggling to stand upright, Max having trouble seeing out of a black eye and Cassidy on the limp, the Indians were missing the team harmony that had carried them so far.

The Wolverines, like the predators they were named for, sprang at their weakened prey. Their confidence soared and they clicked for three fast goals. Marty tried to make kick saves on two of them and was a split second too late. And he had trouble getting to his feet after both. Willie Wheeler dashed in from the wing to deke Marty on the third goal.

Kennedy was tempted to make a goaltending change, but when he looked down the bench, Molly Bright was still sobbing. And she was biting her nails.

"Hang in there, Marty," yelled the coach.

Marty did and made four spectacular saves in a row, preventing the game from becoming a rout.

The period ended with the Wolverines in front by a 4–2 score.

"I've never been in a dressing room so quiet," Max said to Marty during the intermission.

Marty peeled half an orange, handed a slice to Max and hurled the peel against the wall.

"Your eye looks awful," he observed when he took a close look at his brother's face. "And my back is killing me. But we've got to find a way to win this game."

"You're right, Marty. And we will win it. We can't give up. I don't see a quitter in this room, do you?"

Marty looked around. He saw the strained faces of Trudy, Clarence, Kelly, Sammy, Elmo and the rest of his teammates. He noticed the tortured look on Cassidy's face. He saw Coach Kennedy moving around the room, uttering words of encouragement in each player's ear. He realized how much he enjoyed being with this group, and how fortunate he was to be a member of such a team. He loved them all. And he knew that Max did, too.

Coach Kennedy didn't give them much in the way of a team pep talk, but his message registered. "Fellows, ability is what you're capable of doing," he said, emphasizing each word. "Motivation determines what you can do. And attitude determines how well you can do it. Now go out there and give me all that you've got."

There was a whoop from across the room. Clarence was on his feet, shouting, "Come on, you chaps! And Trudy and Molly! Up and at 'em, I say! We're 20 minutes from a championship and a trip to Montreal. Let's not let those ugly Wolverines steal it away from us."

Others joined in, slapping each other on their shoulder pads, shouting excitedly.

"Let's go! Let's get 'em! We can do it!"

Steve Kennedy smiled broadly. He'd heard

similar words before from similar players on similar teams. He could always detect when the words were truly sincere and when they were merely shouts of false bravado. Tonight, he was certain that the words were truly sincere.

"Then go do it, team!" he shouted, clapping his hands and throwing open the dressing room door.

The fans were settled. Many were on the edges of their seats. None wanted to miss a second of the final period.

Steve Kennedy took his place behind the players' bench. He was nervous. Twenty minutes to play and his club was behind by a pair of goals. *Plenty of time*, he thought. *There's still a chance.*

The Wolverines skated out, and he thought they looked a little leg-weary. They had skated miles to score four goals. And miles more chasing Max and his linemates around the ice. And they'd taken a thumping from Clarence. How he loved to hit!

The Wolverines took more bumps from the opening faceoff. Every time one of them touched the puck he paid for it with a check. Finally, they began to fall back and play a defensive game. It was as if they were saying, "All right, you Indians. We've got the two-goal lead. We dare you to snatch it away from us."

When I was young, we called it kitty-bar-the-door hockey, Kennedy thought. *I never did find out why.*

Then he noticed Clarence flying away with the puck.

If there was one thing Clarence enjoyed, it was skating room. The former figure skater loved to display his agility and expertise on the blades. With the Wolverines lined up along their own blue line, Clarence circled his net. He came right down the middle and hopped over his team's blue line— as if it were about to trip him up. He hopped again over the red line—higher this time. His erratic moves seemed to freeze his opponents. They'd never seen anyone leap three feet in the air at centre ice. The Wolverine defence closed ranks, making sure Clarence had no room to slip between them. So he soared right over them. Shoving the puck between them, Clarence electrified the crowd with a leap of at least six feet in the air— right over the heads and shoulders of the open-mouthed defenders. He landed expertly behind them, ice chips flying, and retrieved the rolling puck.

"Blimey! It worked!" he shouted with joy. Then he scampered in on goal, deked Prentice with a nifty move and fired the puck into the upper corner of the net.

He earned a thunderous ovation.

"I thought I'd seen everything in hockey," Kennedy said in Max's ear. "But I've never seen a goal like that. He leaped like a billy goat."

125

"Or a kangaroo," Max said, chuckling. "It's a wonder he didn't crack his head on the rafters."

Momentum was with the Indians now. Clarence had seen to that.

"We need a goal to tie," Trudy shouted from the bench.

"And two goals to win," Steve Kennedy muttered. "If we can just keep the pressure on. And if Lady Luck stays with us."

But the fickle lady suddenly deserted the Indians. Max fed Kelly Jackson a perfect pass, and Jackson darted in on goal. But he was tripped up by Lindsay and crashed into the goal post. "Penalty! Penalty!" Kennedy bellowed. But no penalty was called and Jackson had to be helped off the ice. Kennedy howled in frustration.

Wheeler, the canny Wolverine centre, saw an opportunity. While Jackson was being assisted off the ice, he skated over and stood at the end of the Indians' bench. He had noticed a couple of water bottles sitting on the rail. When the referee turned his back, Wheeler reached out with his stick and knocked the bottles on the ice. One of them hit the referee.

"Hey, Ref," he hollered. "Kennedy just threw some water bottles at you."

The ref picked up the bottles, clearly marked "Indians," and glared at the fuming coach.

"Two-minute bench penalty," he barked. "Delay of game."

Max had seen it all but the angry referee turned a deaf ear to any explanations.

"You weasel," he shouted at Wheeler. "You'll pay for that."

Wheeler just laughed.

Sammy Fox had also seen Wheeler's sneaky trick. He followed the referee to the penalty timekeeper, trying to explain, hoping the man would listen to reason.

The referee wheeled around and said, "All right, wise guy. Since you're here by the box, hop in."

"What for?" cried Sammy.

"For gettin' on my nerves," was the answer. "A ten-minute misconduct should cool you off."

Kennedy hurled his hat in the air. He'd just lost two first-line players and he himself had been penalized for Wheeler's sneaky trick. The momentum his team had enjoyed had suddenly vanished.

Kennedy wisely called a timeout.

His players gathered at the bench, and he spoke to them quietly. "I'm sorry, team. I shouldn't have lost my temper. What's done is done and now we're behind the eight ball. We're two men short and we need a goal badly—just to tie. I'm going to move Clarence up to play on left wing with Max. They'll be our penalty killers—with Cassidy and Leblanc on defence. Trudy, you'll take Kelly Jackson's place on the right side when the penalties are over."

When play resumed, the Wolverines tore into the Indians with a rush that saw half a dozen players sprawled on the ice in front of Marty. But Marty came up with the puck, and when the whistle blew he calmly handed it to the referee.

From the corner faceoff, Max snared the puck and drifted it high down the ice, killing off a few seconds.

Wheeler raced back for it and led another rush into the Indians' zone. But Max was waiting for him. When Wheeler looked up to admire his pass to a winger, Max threw his shoulder and hip into him, sending him hurtling back out over the blue line. He slid on his pants almost to centre ice and lay there, gasping. Cassidy stole the puck and flipped it down the ice, giving Max time to skate over to Wheeler, who was still dazed.

"That's for your water-bottle trick, weasel," Max growled.

On the next rush by the Wolverines, Max trapped the puck along the boards and heard Clarence shout, "Max! Max!"

Clarence was breaking up centre and moving fast. Max threaded the puck between the legs of two Wolverines and hit the tape on Clarence's stick. The big fellow streaked over centre, chased by his opponents. But they had no chance of catching him. Clarence ripped a low shot to the corner, past the outstretched pad of Porky Prentice. The light flashed. Tie game.

Steve Kennedy would say later, "That old barn shook when Clarence scored. No kidding. I could feel it."

There was still a minute of penalty time remaining, but the shorthanded goal by Clarence took a lot of the wind out of the Wolverine's sails. And perhaps punctured their hull as well.

Soon the clubs were back at even strength, and it was a well-rested Trudy Reeves who stunned the visitors in the final minute of play. Max fought hard to get the puck out of the zone and then passed to Clarence on the left wing. He skimmed a long pass to Trudy on the right side. Trudy fed Max a pass and he took the puck over the line. Trudy, with a great burst of speed, legged it around a defender, just in time to take a perfect flip pass from Max. Trudy was in the clear, and she knew there was no time to lose. She looked up, saw an open corner and rifled the puck into the net. It was the go-ahead goal.

"The old barn not only shook, it did a little dance," Kennedy would say later. "I'm surprised the walls didn't come tumbling down."

The Indians mobbed Trudy. Debris littered the ice—hats, gloves, programs, cow bells, even a set of false teeth.

With only two seconds on the clock, there was no attempt to remove the debris, although Marty scooped up a lot of it in front of his net to create a barrier—just in case. There was a final faceoff at centre ice, and two seconds later, the game was over.

Fans jumped the boards and raced over to congratulate their heroes. Trudy was hoisted onto the shoulders of a dozen fans and carried around the rink.

The visitors showed good sportsmanship. They lined up and shook hands with the victors. When Max gripped Wheeler's hand he said, "No hard feelings, pal. Sorry I called you a weasel."

Wheeler said, "Hey, it may become my new nickname." He smiled a gap-toothed smile. "You're a great player, Mitchell. And you're brother is, too. A pleasure to play against. Good luck in Montreal."

"Thanks, pal," Max said. "Have a good summer."

Max hugged Trudy and told her what an asset she'd been to the team.

"I was so afraid I'd let you down, Max," she confessed. "I worried I wouldn't be good enough."

"You were plenty good enough," he said. "Good enough to score the biggest goal of the season." Impulsively, he gave her a big kiss.

"Hey, hey! Hockey players don't kiss each other." It was Clarence who put both arms around them to hug them both.

"Clarence, you were wonderful," Trudy gushed.

"You were indeed," Max added, slapping his teammate on the back. "I've got to get up to Thunder Valley. See what they put in the water up there."

"It's not the water, it's the men in the mill. If you want to play hockey with those birds and survive, you're got to learn to take care of yourself."

CHAPTER 12
BIG DISAPPOINTMENT, BIG SURPRISE

As champions of the Northern League, the Indians waited anxiously for their invitation to come to Montreal for the annual junior playoffs for the national championship.

But no invitation came.

Puzzled by the delay, Coach Kennedy called Mr. Taylor at the mill to discuss the matter. He was shocked to learn that Taylor no longer worked there.

He called Mrs. Gray for an explanation, and she told him, "I fired Mr. Taylor yesterday, Steve. I have evidence it was he who took 1,000 dollars from the company cash box. I trusted him and he betrayed me."

"That's shocking news, Mrs. Gray. Is Taylor still in town?"

"No, Steve. He left immediately for Hartley—after I threatened to lay charges. The Mayor of Hartley, Amos Billings, is Mr. Taylor's brother-in-law. Mayor Billings has found a job for Mr. Taylor."

"I expected to hear from Mayor Billings by now,"

Steve told Mrs. Gray, "to confirm our place in the junior championships. He's the president of our league, as you know. There's something funny going on here. I'll get back to you."

Steve Kennedy immediately called Mayor Billings in Hartley.

"I've been waiting for a call from you," he said curtly. "My team is ready to leave for Montreal. Why the delay?"

The Mayor's reply stunned the coach.

"You're not going to Montreal or anywhere else," he said coldly. "The Hartley team is going in your place."

"What!" shouted Steve.

"I said Hartley is going to represent the Northern League," Amos Billings repeated. Steve pictured him smirking as he spoke.

"But that can't be," Steve responded. "We won the league title, not Hartley."

"No, you didn't," Billings stated. "You broke the rules. You used ineligible players. A representative of each team in the league met today and voted unanimously to suspend your team."

"That's impossible," Steve howled into the telephone. "What ineligible players?"

"Clarence Clarington-Clarke for one," was Billings' response. "You never officially got permission to use him as one of your imports."

"But I called you about him," the coach said, his

voice rising. "You said you wanted a Brit in the league."

"That's right," replied Billings. "But that agreement was verbal. You should have followed up with a written request to use Clarence. And then there's Trudy Reeves..."

"Trudy?" Kennedy bellowed. "What about Trudy?" Steve Kennedy's cheeks were red with anger.

"There's a league rule that one of our committee members discovered only today—no girls allowed. And another one states that no handicapped players shall be allowed to play."

"I assume that you're referring to Charlie Chin," Kennedy growled. "Well, we don't consider him handicapped. Tell me, who discovered these asinine rules? And how come the vote was unanimous? Who represented our club at this meeting? If I'd been there, I'd never have voted us out."

Billings chuckled and replied, "Mr. James Taylor represented your team, even though he no longer resides in your community. He discovered the rules in question. He told the committee members, 'As a man of great integrity I apologize for the Indians' behaviour and their flouting of the league rules.' He even apologized for you, Mr. Kennedy, and the Mitchell brothers. He said those two kids persuaded you to break the rules and all of you now regret your actions."

"What bull!" Kennedy snarled. "It's pretty obvious to me that Taylor—your brother-in-law—is just getting even for what happened here. I'll have Mrs. Gray call you to tell you that Taylor no longer represents our team. And she'll put it in writing."

"No need," said the Mayor. "Taylor resigned as your team manager right after today's meeting. He'll be joining our team in a similar capacity."

Kennedy slammed down the phone, but not before adding a warning. "Better keep your money in a safe place, Billings—with Taylor around."

Kennedy rushed over to Merry Mabel's, where he found Max, Marty and Trudy sitting in a booth. He delivered the bad news.

"How could they do this to us?" wailed Marty. "We won the title fair and square."

"I never liked Mr. Taylor very much," Trudy said. "I know he resented the fact that you let me play for the Indians."

"And I know there was something funny going on between him and those two clowns, Oliver and Riddell," Kennedy snorted. "I think he gave them the money he stole."

"So we've lost our chance to pummel the fancy teams from the big cities—just like we did last year," said Max. "It's really disappointing. The students on the team have already been granted permission to miss some school and the mill workers have been given a couple of weeks off.

The town was really behind us. Folks were counting on us being in Montreal."

"I always wanted to see the Montreal Forum," Marty said sadly. "Now I guess I'll have to wait until I play in the NHL—with the Canadiens, of course."

Clarence was bitterly disappointed when Max and Marty called him in Thunder Valley to relay the news. "I just heard about it on the radio," he said. "It's depressing, isn't it? I was hoping to be the first Brit to play in the junior finals. By the way, did you know a British team just won the gold medal at the 1936 Olympic games in Germany? It was a huge upset over Canada. In England everyone is talking about it. My pater, I mean my father, has become a big fan of the game."

Max chuckled. "Clarence, most of the players on the British team were Canadians who'd immigrated from England when they were young. They were invited back to play for England because they were born there."

"That may be, but the only thing that matters to the Brits is they won the gold. Sorry, fellows, I've got to hang up—I have a call coming in from England. Tell you what. Meet me at Merry Mabel's tomorrow night. And bring Coach Kennedy with you, okay? Seven o'clock. Goodbye."

"I wonder why Clarence wants to meet with us?" Max said, after hanging up the phone.

"We'll find out soon enough," Marty answered.

The gloom that had settled over Indian River was lifted dramatically shortly after Clarence came to town.

"All right, here's my scheme," he told them over chocolate sundaes at Merry Mabel's. "The hockey officials over here snubbed us, right? Well, I figured we should have been invited to play in Montreal. And I said to myself, if not Montreal, where else could we play?"

"What are you getting at, Clarence?" Steve Kennedy asked. "The season's over. Done like dinner. There's nowhere else to play."

Clarence smiled. "Perhaps there is, Coach. How about overseas? I've been calling England, and the officials over there loved my story about a team of ragamuffins winning the title here. They were excited to learn a Brit was on the club. And a female player, too. And a couple of bona fide Indians. We've been invited to spend a week in London, all expenses paid, playing a couple of exhibition games—perhaps before royalty."

"That's incredible!" Max exploded. "Unbelievable!"

"Wow! A trip to England!" Marty hollered, turning heads in Merry Mabel's. "How in the world did you manage that, Clarence?"

"I never told you this, but my pater, my father,

is a Lord over there. He even plays polo with the royal family. You might say he has...er...a few connections."

"You're full of surprises, Clarence," Steve Kennedy said, shaking his head.

"That's not all, Coach," Clarence said, flashing another secretive smile. "We've also been invited to play a game on the Olympic ice in Garmisch, Germany. In the same rink where the Olympics were held. The German chancellor, Adolf Hitler, has issued a special invitation to us."

"Isn't that kind of scary?" Max asked. "Hitler's a bad guy, a dictator preparing for another big war. My dad says he's really anti-Semitic."

"What's that mean?" Marty asked.

"It means he hates the Jews. Some have fled the country. Others have been put in prison camps."

Clarence sighed. "It's true he's a nasty man. But in England we're all hoping that he'll come to his senses and that war will never come. Anyway, we'll only be there two days. And the Germans will pay expenses and then some."

The meeting at Merry Mabel's led to a second meeting involving all the parents of the school-aged players and other interested parties. The Mayor loved the idea of a hockey trip overseas and supported it. So did most of the parents.

Harry Mitchell spoke. "Folks, the players will miss some school—maybe as much as a month.

And the mill workers will have to get a leave of absence. But the trip will be a once-in-a-lifetime experience. It will be hugely educational. Amy and I endorse it 100 percent."

"Especially if all expenses are paid," another parent shouted out.

Molly Bright was the only member of the team to decline the invitation. "Sorry, everyone, but I get seasick. I shudder to think of crossing the ocean. I can't do it."

In the end, the overseas' junket won universal approval. Mrs. Gray had the final word.

"I'm proud to announce that the Mill will make a donation of 1,000 dollars to cover any additional expenses. The Mill will also provide a tutor for the players who want to keep up with their studies. The publicity we receive from being the team sponsor will make it all worthwhile."

And so, two weeks later, after some frantic efforts to obtain passports and other documentation, the Indian River hockey players found themselves on a train to New York City where they would stay overnight. They strolled through the heart of the busy city, gawking at the tall buildings and the mass of humanity that dashed about in all directions. They visited the Statue of Liberty and ate in a restaurant where the waiters sang songs in Italian.

The next morning, they boarded the largest ship any of them had ever seen—the *Normandie*—an ocean liner that was a veritable floating palace.

"It's longer than three football fields," Max told Marty, "and it weighs almost 80,000 tons. It's the biggest ship ever built."

"Wow!" said Marty as they walked up the broad gangplank. "She was launched less than a year ago. And she's got a movie theatre that seats 400 people. This is going to be the trip of a lifetime."

The *Normandie* whisked them across the endless expanse of ocean in a few days, and soon they were ensconced in posh rooms at the fashionable Empress Hotel in London.

"I can't believe this is happening," Max said to Marty. "We play our first game tomorrow against the British Olympic team—the gold-medal winners."

"What a thrill it would be to beat them," Marty said. "Do you think they'd give us their gold medals if we did?"

"Not a chance," Max said.

The game at Harringay Stadium drew a full house. Clarence's father, Lord Clarington-Clarke, arranged for the Duke and Duchess of York to be in attendance.

When the teams lined up to shake hands with the royal couple, Marty got confused.

"Max, am I supposed to curtsey—like the little

girl did who handed the Duchess some flowers?"

"Certainly," Max answered, straight-faced. "I hope you know how."

"Gosh, I don't," Marty stammered. "Now what am I gonna do?"

Max wouldn't let the practical joke go any further. He didn't want his brother to be a laughingstock on this special occasion. "Just bow," he told Marty.

Marty not only bowed deeply when he took the hand of the Duchess, but impulsively kissed her gloved fingertips, drawing a huge round of applause from the crowd.

He returned, grinning. "I guess they know now we've got good manners in the North Country," he quipped.

The game was fast and exciting. The Olympic-team players wanted to prove to their fans that the gold medal they'd captured in Germany a month earlier was no fluke. Meanwhile the visitors were eager to prove that they belonged on the same ice as the medal winners.

There was a great roar of applause when Clarence was announced as the starting centre for the Indians. And another ovation when a female— Trudy Reeves—replaced him after his first shift.

"By Jove, she has spunk!" Max heard a spectator proclaim.

Max graciously agreed to centre a third line, knowing that the crowd's interest was mainly focused on Clarence and Trudy.

And while Clarence and Trudy each scored a goal to stake the visitors to a 2–0 lead, earning much applause, it was Max who dominated the game with a four-goal outburst that helped sink the Olympians 7–4. Sammy Fox and Elmo Swift assisted on all four of his goals.

After the game, a photographer from a London tabloid wanted Sammy and Elmo to pose brandishing tomahawks and wearing feathers in their hair. He planned to stage a shot of the Indian lads pretending to scalp the referee.

"Go away!" Sammy said harshly. "We're not savages. Such a photo would be an insult to our people."

Undeterred, the photographer used doctored head and shoulder photos of Sammy and Elmo in his paper prior to the second game. A staff artist painted in headdresses of war feathers, and the writer headlined his article "Savages on Ice":

> Two savage Indians will display their skill on skates against the British Olympic Team at the Wembley Arena tonight. Elmo Swift and Sammy Running Fox, who live in igloos in the winter and teepees in the summer in North America and whose diet consists of raw meat from game killed by bows and arrows, will be in the Indians' lineup for the second and final game of their time in England. The

two players refused to wear the traditional head covering of feathers that is part of their everyday wardrobe at home. They spoke to this reporter in their own language, which consists mainly of grunts. Patrons attending the game tonight should exercise extreme caution and not approach the Indians for fear of being attacked and possibly scalped. It's rumoured the two players have toma-hawks hidden under their hockey apparel...

"What rot!" Sammy exclaimed when he read the column. He threw the paper down. "Eskimos live in igloos, not Indians. And we now use rifles to kill game, not bows and arrows."

"And we don't speak in grunts," Elmo Swift said disapprovingly. "But hiding a tomahawk in my underwear is a good idea," he added in jest. "It might come in handy during a fight."

"Don't let the British press upset you," Clarence told Sammy and Elmo. "They'll write and print anything if it sells papers."

Sammy's anger and determination led to a hat trick—three goals—in the second game. After his third goal late in the match, he skated by the press box and gave the journalists sitting there a tomahawk chop. The crowd loved it and cheered wildly. Max added a pair of goals and the Indians won 6–4. Clarence capped the evening with an empty net goal with two seconds to play. He circled the rink at the final whistle, throwing kisses to the fans.

"Thank you! Thank you!" he cried out, proud to be recognized for what he was—an outstanding hockey player, one of the best ever produced by England.

"Next time you're looking for players for your Olympic team, don't forget to look in the North Country," he suggested to reporters. "That's where I'll be. And now we're off to Germany."

Flashbulbs popped and fans gathered around to pump his hand and pat his back. "I hope we meet Hitler," he added. "I'll tell him flat out to give up those plans of his to dominate the world."

CHAPTER 13

ON TO GERMANY

A large ferryboat transported the Indian River hockey club across the English Channel to the coast of France. After passing through French customs and immigration, the team boarded a train, which swept them across France and up to the border of Germany.

There, German soldiers checked their hockey bags and documents. They examined personal belongings closely. One of them unzipped Marty's hockey bag and almost gagged. He waved a hand in front of his nose. The mood of the soldiers was suspicious and grim, not at all friendly like the French. And the Germans were armed with machine guns.

"Our German boys are ready to give you arrogant North Americans a hockey lesson you will long remember," one of them sneered. "You are young. Our players are polished veterans. They have wills of steel, and muscles to match. You will be like puppy dogs going up against fierce German shepherds."

Marty couldn't resist. "But can they skate?" he blurted.

Luckily, the burly soldier didn't hear him and waved them through.

Garmisch proved to be a wondrous winter resort high in the Bavarian mountains. The players were booked into rooms in a hotel overlooking a picturesque ski hill. It was said that Adolf Hitler had a mountain residence nearby where he sometimes retreated to plot ways and means of crushing neighbouring countries and innocent people.

After the team was settled, and following a team meeting, the players practiced on the outdoor Olympic ice surface. The rink of natural ice was well maintained, but to the players' surprise, the rink boards were only a foot high. Pucks flew into snowbanks bordering the playing surface with ridiculous ease.

Unheated dressing rooms—one for each team— were flimsy structures located under the stands. Trudy dressed in her room at the resort and walked through the hard-packed snow to the rink.

Many teams might have complained about playing a game outdoors, with wind and snow to worry about. Not the Indians. They were accustomed to freezing temperatures and ruts in the ice. It reminded them of thousands of games they had played in their younger days.

"Reminds me of playing on the river ice back home," Sammy said. "It's hard to believe they played Olympic games on such a rink."

Steve Kennedy spoke. "There's no question Hitler is upset because his Olympic team lost to the British," he said. "His players are in disgrace. They want to salvage some respect by walloping us if they can."

"Does the German team have a star player, Coach?" Marty asked. "A scorer I should worry about?"

"Yes. His name is Rudi Ball. And guess what? He's a Jewish player. Ball was living in exile in France, but now his nation needs him. Hitler persuaded him to come back for the Olympics. He's using Ball as a symbol to show that Germany is not against the Jews. It's a farce, of course. All Jews in Germany are in great peril. Now that Ball has returned he may never be able to go back to France."

"Or anywhere else," added Max.

Despite the cold weather and the threat of snow, a huge crowd turned out for the game against the German Olympic team.

"I had no idea there was so much interest in our little team from the North Country," Max said to Steve Kennedy before they went out on the ice.

Kennedy chuckled. "A lot of true hockey fans are in the crowd," he said. "The rest of the seats are filled with Hitler's party members. He wants every one filled—and what Hitler wants, he gets."

The German players received a long, loud ovation when they skated out. Ball, number seven, was a graceful skater with quick bursts of speed. Even in the warm-up, he showed great skill at handling the puck.

When Ball circled the ice he deliberately skated alongside Max. Max could see fear in his eyes.

"I want to speak with you after the game," Rudi Ball said, talking without turning his head. "Meet me behind your dressing room."

Before Max could reply, Ball had skated away and the game began.

If the Indians had expected a gentlemanly game with the Germans, they were in for a surprise.

Adolf Hitler himself attended. He made a grand entrance as hundreds of arms rose high in the air, saluting the dictator with the small moustache. He sat in a special box, surrounded by grim-faced aides.

"What a silly looking moustache," Marty commented.

"Hush," Max said.

Kennedy called his players to the bench before the opening whistle. "Fellows, we might have been better off to stay in England. The referee just told me that Hitler sent one of his flunkeys to the German dressing room. He told them they'd better win today—or else." Kennedy made a cutting motion across his throat. "And he told Rudi Ball to score some goals or he'd wind up in a camp with a lot of other Jews."

Marty spoke up. "So you're saying to watch out for some rough play. Anything goes, right?"

"That's right, Marty. I'm sorry about this. I should have anticipated it."

"Don't worry, Coach," Max said. "We'll keep our heads up. These guys can't be any tougher than some of the miners and lumberjacks we've faced back home."

The referee blew his whistle and the game was underway.

The Germans won the faceoff and bulled their way into the Indians' zone. What they lacked in finesse they made up for with aggressive play: slashing, hooking, rough bodychecking and even some spearing. Karl "the Beast" Buller, their huge defenceman, billed as "Europe's toughest player" was particularly mean-spirited. He nailed Max with a check from behind and sent him over the boards into a snowbank. Max wiped snow from his face and jumped back over the boards. He made note of Buller's number. And of the smirk on his face.

When he turned to the referee with a "What, no penalty?" look, the referee smirked, too.

Buller added insult to injury seconds later by

scoring the first goal of the game—on a long shot that was screened. Marty never had a chance.

Then Rudi Ball displayed some fancy stickhandling inside the Indians' zone and scored on his own rebound.

The German crowd made Clarence a target with their derisive jeers.

"English, go home!" someone shouted. Clarence just grinned.

And Trudy, so often applauded for playing a man's game and playing it to perfection, was greeted with disdain.

"Go bake cookies!" someone cried.

"You want to play with men, grow a beard!" shouted another.

Trudy finished her shift and nudged Max at the bench.

"I won't grow a beard, but I might settle for a neat little moustache—like Hitler's," she quipped, laughing. "I bet they'd like me then."

"That's the spirit," Max replied, putting one arm around Trudy and waving the other at the crowd, showing his support for a teammate. "Remember what we learned as kids, sticks and stones..."

The period ended with the Indians trailing 2–0.

During the first intermission it began to snow. And the wind picked up, blowing into the faces of the Indians.

The German club played defensively throughout

the second period, protecting their two-goal lead. They hoped their goaltender, Hans Hermann, would earn a shutout. Hitler grew bored with the emphasis on defence and left midway through the period in a limousine. Play halted while the crowd cheered his exit, right arms upraised.

"They either love that guy or they're scared to death of him," Max observed.

Time and again the Indians swept over the German blue line, only to be tackled or bodied to the ice, chopped across the shins or crosschecked about the shoulders. Each time there was an obvious infraction, the referee appeared to be looking up, studying the sky, wondering how long it would be before he was home again, getting warm in front of the fire.

At the end of two periods, the score remained 2–0.

"Come on, fellows!" Max pleaded in the cramped dressing room. "Let's not go home without a goal. Let's beat these guys. We all know the referee is blind or biased or both. And the snow on the ice is piling up. Let's show this crowd what we're made of in the final period."

His inspirational pep talk may have been a factor in what happened over the final 20 minutes of play. Max himself led off with a sensational rink-length dash that ended with a blistering shot on goal. Hans Hermann got a piece of it with his glove, but the puck dropped just over the line—clearly a goal.

But the goal judge waved it off.

"No goal! No goal!" he shouted. "Puck did not cross the goal line."

Annoyed and frustrated, Max slapped his stick on the ice.

"Two minute penalty," shouted the referee, waving Max to the penalty box. "That was unsportsmanlike."

While Max was cooling off in the penalty box, Clarence did some masterful stickhandling, keeping the puck away from the Germans and frustrating any semblance of a power play.

Max applauded from the box while the crowd shrieked, "Go home, English! Go home!"

Soon only half a period was left to play. Then five minutes. With an inch of snow covering the ice, Marty had trouble seeing the puck. He scrambled to make a save, and then spotted Max along the far boards. Marty shovelled the puck ahead to his brother and Max streaked away with it. Snow flew up from the blade of his stick as he crossed the German blue line. Buller—the Beast—was waiting there, bracing himself and preparing to smash into Max. He lunged headfirst, his mouth twisted in a snarl. Max slipped the puck through Buller's legs and nailed him with his shoulder at the same time. Buller's big nose spurted blood, and he cried out in pain and tumbled to the ice. No doubt Max would have been penalized but the referee was busy wiping flakes of snow from his eyes and didn't see Max's elbow.

Max didn't look back. He snapped up the loose puck and raced in on Hermann. A head fake, an expert deke with his arms and wrists and the puck slid into the net behind the stumbling goalie. This time the goal judge could not wave it off. The Indians trailed by one.

What a lift that goal gave the Indians!

From the faceoff, it was Trudy's turn to dazzle.

She won the draw and skimmed the puck across the ice to Sammy Fox. Sammy moved over the blue line and flipped the puck back to Trudy, who darted between the two defencemen and slashed a quick shot into the corner of the net. Tie game!

Hermann fished the puck out of the net in shock. His shutout was long gone and his team's best defenceman, Buller, was nursing a bloody nose on the bench, through for the day. His mates had punished and pummelled the visitors throughout the game and they had kept on coming.

There was a minute to play. The referee was determined to give the home team every opportunity to score. Max knocked Rudi Ball off stride near the Indians' blue line and the referee blew his whistle.

"Penalty shot!"

"A disgraceful call!" Steve Kennedy bellowed from the bench. He threw his hat down and trampled it.

The referee pulled a pair of earmuffs from his pocket and slipped them on, indicating he would hear no more criticism from the visitors. He placed the puck at centre ice and motioned to Ball.

Ball was a clever player, a hard shooter and a natural goal-scorer. He moved in swiftly and spotted an opening to the corner of the net. He went for it—shooting hard. But Marty had given him the opening, knowing he could get a pad over in time. And he did, blocking Ball's drive just as the puck seemed certain to fly into the net.

Ball threw his arms in the air in frustration. Marty gave him a pat on the back as he skated past. "Nice try, pal," he said.

Max looked over at the clock. Twenty seconds to play. He fed a pass to Clarence and took a return pass. He dashed into the German zone, and was about to shoot from a sharp angle. Then he changed his mind. He whirled and saw Clarence racing straight down the middle. Max drove a hard pass directly onto the stick of the flying Brit. Clarence let out a whoop and shot a bullet at Hermann. The goalie never saw the puck. The netting bulged and the red light flashed.

The Indians had won the game in the last second of play!

The referee was tempted to nullify the goal, claiming that time had expired. But obviously it hadn't. He hesitated, and then shrugged. He had tried his best to make it easy for the German club to win. If Herr Hitler decided to send him to the coal mines, so be it. He turned his back and skated off the ice.

The German team followed him. Only Rudi Ball and a couple of others remained to shake hands with the North Country team.

When Rudi shook hands with Max, he whispered, "Don't forget. Behind your dressing room. In 20 minutes."

CHAPTER 14

A DARING ESCAPE

Max and Marty stood in the shadows of the small dressing room underneath the grandstand at the Garmisch rink.

"Wonder what this is all about?" Marty whispered, stamping his feet in the snow.

Moments later, Rudi Ball slipped around the corner and joined them.

"I must speak quickly," he said. "I only have a few minutes. Then they'll come looking for me."

Before Max could ask who "they" were, Rudi continued.

"I am desperate for your help. I only came back to Germany to help the hockey team at the Olympics. I was pressured to come back. Hitler's sports minister told me my relatives here might suffer if I didn't. You boys have no idea how frightened the Jewish people are here in Germany."

"But what can we do for you?" Marty asked. "We're leaving on the train tomorrow."

"Here's my problem," Rudi explained. "I have a relative here, my ten-year-old nephew Alan Ball. I'm hiding him in my room at the hotel. Alan's parents disappeared mysteriously a few weeks ago and friends have been caring for him. When they heard I was here in Garmisch they put Alan on a train and sent him to me. They did not want to be found with a Jewish boy in their home."

"Aren't you going back to France?" Max asked. "Can't you take Alan with you?"

Rudi Ball frowned. "They may not let me go back to France now—even though they promised. They may force me to play more hockey. Or they may send me to a concentration camp. I don't care about myself. But Alan is a special boy—very smart, very well mannered. I must try to get him out of Germany."

"And you want us to sneak him out somehow," Max said.

"Exactly."

"Sounds kinda risky," Marty said.

"I will be honest with you. It is risky. There's no telling what might happen to you if you are found out. But if you get Alan out, you may be saving the life of a boy who will someday become a very important man. To me, you will be heroes."

Max and Marty stared at each other.

"How would we hide him?" Marty asked.

Max replied instantly. "I know—in your

goaltender's bag. It's bigger than most bags. You could carry your goalie pads over your shoulder. Is Alan small?"

"Very small. Less than 100 pounds."

"We could puncture some small air holes for breathing at the end of the bag," Marty suggested. "And throw a couple of jerseys over him. In case someone decides to peek inside. It might work."

"If we're lucky," Max added. "Alan would have to stay in the bag for most of tomorrow," he told Rudi. "He'd be in there until we cross the border into France."

"Alan is very brave," Rudi said. "He will do it. I will give him a sandwich, a bottle of water and a bottle to pee in. I know he can do it." Rudi's face lit up with an expression of hope and relief. "Then you will help me? You will bring my nephew to North America?"

"Hold on," Max said. "We will try to get him out of Germany because his life is at risk here. But after that..." Max put his hands up. "Who knows?"

"I am satisfied," Rudi Ball said. "I will never forget you for this, my brothers in hockey. Never! And someday I will find a way to leave Germany and be reunited with my nephew."

He produced a pencil and paper. "Quick. Write your room number on this. And write down your address in North America. I will come to your room with Alan at six o'clock tomorrow morning."

Rudi Ball reached out and embraced the Mitchell brothers. "You are my champions," he said, and hurried off.

Max and Marty sat next to each other as the train carrying the hockey team raced toward the French border. Their seats faced the end of the car where more than a dozen red hockey bags were piled up—the words "Indian River Hockey Club" stencilled on the sides. They kept a close eye on bag number 30, an extra large bag containing a few team jerseys and a very important ten year old—Alan Ball.

"I hope he doesn't suffocate in there," Marty whispered in Max's ear. "You think I made the air holes big enough?"

"They're plenty big," Max whispered back. "I saw the bag twitch a moment ago so he's still breathing. Another hour and this will all be over."

At six that morning there had been a quiet rapping on their hotel-room door. Rudi Ball stood outside, his arm around the shoulder of a frail young boy. The boy's eyes glistened, partly in fear and partly with excitement. He was obviously aware that this was a day that would change his life forever.

Alan Ball shook hands gently with the Mitchell brothers when he and Rudi were ushered through the door and had closed it behind them.

"Here is Alan's lunch," he said, handing Max a paper bag. "And his water bottle. And here's another bottle. We know what that is for."

"I try not use it," Alan said, struggling with English. He smiled. "But if I do, I make sure put cap on tight after."

Rudi looked at his watch. "I must run. Goodbye, my nephew." He took Alan in his strong arms. "I am asking a lot of you. I am asking you to be a man—at least for today. You can be a boy again tomorrow—when you are safe. Au revoir." He kissed his nephew on the forehead, thanked the Mitchell brothers once again and slipped out the door.

"We have to hurry, too," Max said. "Our train leaves at seven." He turned to Alan. "The station is just across the street. We took our other bags down to the station before you got here. And I told the station master that we have to carry our bags aboard because our school books are in them and we plan to study."

Marty chuckled. "We actually did bring some school books with us. And our tutor is proof that we have to study."

Alan nodded. "I trust. You look after me," he said.

Marty had cleaned out his goaltending bag and had placed a thick towel on the bottom. Aside from his big pads, which he would carry over his shoulder, the rest of his gear was jammed into Max's bag. He nodded at Alan to get in. Alan fit comfortably into the bag with his legs folded up. He placed his mouth close to the breathing holes. Marty carefully folded three or four hockey jerseys and stockings on top of the lad. Then he zipped up the bag, leaving the end of a stocking sticking out. He hoped it would indicate what was inside to a customs or immigration inspector.

Max looked around the room. "Got everything? Let's go," he said. He gripped one strap of the bag and Marty gripped the other. They lifted it easily. There wasn't a peep from Alan. The door closed behind them.

On the station platform, their teammates stood around, hands in their pockets, their breath rising in the morning air. They began to board the train.

Sammy Fox looked over his shoulder and called out, "Almost forgot your bag, did you?"

Max and Marty had agreed not to tell their teammates what was happening.

"Almost, Sammy," he called back. "Good thing I'm strong as a mule. Marty could never have carried all this gear by himself."

At the border, German officials, in full uniform and carrying machine guns, gathered around the hockey players and examined their papers. It appeared that two or three of the gun-toting guards were hockey fans, from the interest they took in the players' sticks and bags.

One of them—an officer with many medals on his chest—approached Max and Marty.

"You were playing hockey in Garmisch?" he asked. "Was that the purpose of your trip?"

"Yes, we were," Max replied. Wisely, he added, "Herr Hitler arranged for it. We played there yesterday against the German Olympic team."

"And who won the game?" the colonel asked. "Our German team is very good, no?"

Marty laughed. "Good enough to beat the pants off us," he lied. "They were dynamite."

The man's eyebrows shot up. "You have dynamite. Where?"

"No, no, no dynamite," Marty said quickly. "It's just an expression. An expression we use back home."

He pulled a hockey puck from his pocket.

"I'm the goalie and these little black things kept piling up in my net. Want one for a souvenir?"

Finally, the German officer chuckled. "I might think you are trying to bribe me. But a simple hockey puck..." He grinned and put it away. "For my boy, he's ten years old."

"So is..." Marty began.

Max said smoothly, "Our brother back home. Ten years old."

The officer nodded at the hockey bags lined up. He said to Marty, "Your bag must be the bigger one—the goalie's bag. Why are you carrying your pads over your shoulder?"

Marty said, "The boys threw their jerseys in my bag, see?" He went over and unzipped the bag a little and pulled out a jersey. "I'm a rookie. They play jokes on the rookies. I have to carry my gear and the jerseys."

The official nodded. "I get it. And those little holes at the end of the bag?"

"Sir, they're air holes. Have you ever smelled inside a hockey bag? It's not pleasant." Marty pinched his nostrils with two fingers and made a face. "We punch holes in them to let the stinky air out."

The official said, "I see. Well, perhaps I'll take a closer look." He started toward the bag and had his hand on the zipper when a commotion broke out.

He spun around to see one of his soldiers pushing Elmo and Sammy ahead of him.

"Herr Colonel, these two hockey players look Jewish to me. Should we detain them? They say they are not Jewish but Indian."

"We are from the Iroquois nation," Sammy Fox explained. "A proud tribe in North America. This man thinks we should be from Delhi or Calcutta if we are Indians."

"You dummy!" the officer said angrily. "Release those boys. I have read about the North American Indian. Let them get back on the train."

He turned to Max and Marty. "You boys carry that bag out of here. I'm finished with you, too."

"Thank you, sir," said Marty.

Max turned to leave with Marty when the officer shouted, "Stop!"

Max turned, a flicker of fear spreading through his stomach.

"Yes?"

The officer took a step forward and pointed at the bag. "There's a piece of stocking sticking out. Tuck it in. And help your poor brother carry his bag. Shame on you for making him carry his goal pads plus all those jerseys."

"Yes, sir," Max said, holding back a sigh of relief. "I'll be glad to give him a hand."

Once the train rumbled into France, the mood lightened. In fact, it was one of celebration.

Alan was released from the bag to the astonishment of the rest of the group. His dramatic escape from Germany became the central story of the trip.

The boy jumped out of the bag and did an impromptu dance, looking around for Max, who realized instantly why the lad was so jumpy.

Alan waved an empty bottle in the air and Max shouted, "This way, Alan, this way to the lavatory."

CHAPTER 15

THE TRIP HOME

"Now we have to worry about how to get Alan out of France and onto the *Normandie*," Max said to Steve Kennedy. "On the return trip to New York the *Normandie* leaves from France, not England."

That's when Clarence stepped forward to save the day. "I'll make calls to London during our next stop," he said. "My father is a close friend of the Prime Minister. He will, as you say in North America, pull some strings. The Prime Minister is disgusted with Hitler. He certainly will be pleased to learn how you helped Alan escape a terrible fate. I'm sure he will talk to the French government and ask for their help. After all, the French will need help from England if a war breaks out."

Clarence was as good as his word. By the time the Indians reached the port city of Brest, a telegram had reached the immigration authorities there. It granted Alan Ball refugee status, which meant he was free to leave for America on the *Normandie*. Clarence's father had even arranged payment for Alan's passage—a generous gesture.

"What will we do with Alan when we reach New York?" Marty asked Max. "He doesn't know a soul in North America."

"I don't know," Max replied thoughtfully. "But things will work out. We may have to take him to Indian River with us."

"Sure. We could bring him home. Won't Mom and Dad be surprised?"

"We'd better phone them from New York. You know Mom. She'll want to vacuum the house if she knows a guest is coming."

On the ship, Max and Marty took time to get to know Alan, who proved to be everything his uncle Rudi had said he was. He was shy, but well mannered and very intelligent. At chess, he beat Steve Kennedy and several passengers who took an interest in him. He studied English every day and was soon able to converse with everyone on board reasonably well.

"And what an appetite he has!" Marty said.

"It's no wonder he has a good appetite. Anyone would who'd grown up like Alan—with just enough food to keep them alive."

In New York, the team stayed overnight at a hotel. Steve Kennedy announced he had a surprise for them.

"The New York Rangers want us to be their guests at a playoff game tonight against the

Bruins. It's their way of thanking us for being such great ambassadors for hockey overseas."

The team was thrilled. None of them had ever seen an NHL game. Tickets had been arranged and their seats were directly in back of the Ranger bench.

In a pre-game ceremony, the North Country players were escorted to centre ice and introduced to the fans. They received a standing ovation when the crowd was told they had defeated both the British and German Olympic teams on their overseas trip.

Max, as team captain, was invited to drop the puck for a ceremonial faceoff. Bill Cook, the Rangers' All-Star, picked up the puck, handed it to Max and said, "I hope we'll see you playing with our club someday, kid. Come to the dressing room after the game and I'll give you my stick."

The game was a thriller, ending in a one-goal victory for the Rangers. The Mitchell brothers had never heard such frantic cheering at a hockey game.

Max, Marty, Trudy and Clarence rushed down to the bowels of the arena after the game and hovered outside the dressing room door.

An attendant appeared. He wore a jacket with a Ranger crest on the sleeve. Max called out, "We're here to see Mr. Cook."

"Then come on in," the man replied, ushering

them in the door. "You too, miss."

Already dressed in their well-pressed suits, snap brim fedoras and highly polished shoes, the Rangers looked like young businessmen, until you got close enough to see the scar tissue on their faces. There were lines where stitches had closed past wounds. Max noticed one player pluck some dentures from a paper cup and insert them smoothly into a mouth where real teeth had once stood tall.

Bill Cook came over and presented Max with a stick autographed by the players. Marty looked on enviously.

Cook called across the room, "Hey, goolie," he said to big Chuck Rayner, the Ranger goaltender. "Get one of your old war clubs for this young fellow."

Rayner came over and shook Marty's hand. "You a goalie, kid?"

"I sure am, Mr. Rayner."

"Then I'll sign one of my goal sticks for you." He took a marker and wrote on the blade of the stick, "To my pal Marty. A future NHL star."

Marty was all but speechless, but he did manage to stammer, "Thanks, Mr. Rayner."

Clarence and Trudy, meanwhile, were making the rounds, shaking hands with every player and getting autographs.

Lester Patrick took a special interest in Trudy.

"I'm glad to hear you play the game," he told

her. "My sisters all played when I was young."

"Do you think there'll ever be women players in the NHL, Mr. Patrick?" Trudy asked.

The hockey legend hesitated. "Perhaps, Trudy. In a few years, maybe. A woman goalie might have the best chance. Heck, female players may even form a pro league of their own someday. I wouldn't bet against it."

The white-haired manager handed autographed sticks to Trudy and Clarence. Then he said to Clarence, "Steve Kennedy tells me you're an outstanding player, and Steve knows hockey. Our scouts will be watching you." He winked at Trudy. "This fellow's not a cream puff, is he, Trudy? Cream puffs don't cut it in the NHL."

Trudy laughed and said, "Clarence is no cream puff. Far from it."

Clarence said, "I used to be a Cream Puff, Mr. Patrick. But not anymore. That was just the name on my jersey. Ask any of the German players we met—I left my mark on a few of them."

"Good man," said Patrick, patting Clarence on the back. "Be sure and say hello to our Ching Johnston, the NHL's toughest player. He's the old bald guy over there." Johnston laughed, his shining dome reflecting light, his devilish smile indicating his love for the game, his willingness to fight for every puck.

"Wow! What a privilege!" Marty gasped as they

left the room. "What a great bunch of men!"

"I'll say! It was a thrill, wasn't it?" Max said. "It was awesome. What did you think, Clarence?"

"I've got a new idol, mates. That Ching Johnston better watch out. I'm out to take his place."

The next morning they boarded the train that carried them back home—back to the North Country. Their long journey was almost over.

To their amazement, half the town turned out to welcome them back to Indian River. The station platform threatened to cave in under the weight of the parents and friends who greeted the Indians.

Harry and Amy Mitchell rushed over to hug Max and Marty.

"We're so proud of you boys," their mother gushed, kissing them on both cheeks while their father pumped their hands and pounded their backs. The other players were treated with similar affection. Mrs. Gray embraced Clarence and promised him a new job at the mill as assistant supervisor.

"But who'll I be assisting, Auntie?" Clarence asked.

"Why, Steve Kennedy," she replied. "I believe he'll make an ideal manager, don't you?"

"Absolutely," said Clarence. "It's a promotion for both of us."

Mr. and Mrs. Reeves pushed their way through

the crowd and hugged Trudy until she thought her ribs would crack.

Sammy's folks and other natives from the Tumbling Waters reserve raised Sammy and Elmo onto their shoulders and paraded them up and down the platform, which shook but did not splinter or cave.

Almost lost in the commotion was Alan Ball, who looked on in amazement at the sight. Then Max scooped him up and introduced him to Uncle Jake and Harry and Amy Mitchell. Big Fella, the Mitchells' big husky, jumped up and licked Alan on the nose.

Amy Mitchell hugged Alan. "We've heard so much about you, Alan. You'll be staying with us for a while. Now go with Max and Marty. The Mayor has a special treat for you and the players."

The Mayor had arranged a parade up Main Street in open convertibles, and the players scrambled aboard. People came from far and wide to salute their hockey heroes, to wave and call out as each car passed. The high school band played lively marches and a drum majorette strutted in front, expertly tossing a baton high in the air every few paces, drawing "oohs" and "aahs" from small children lining the sidewalks.

Alan Ball sat between Max and Marty in the back of a Buick on loan from Wally Beck the Buick dealer. People had heard about Alan's thrilling escape and cheered him loudly. He grinned shyly and waved to all of these nice strangers.

The Mayor had further arranged a banquet honouring the Indians in the town hall. The lucky ticket holders jammed into the building, and after a buffet banquet the Mayor spoke glowingly of the Indians.

"We're right proud of you boys—and Trudy—for what you've done for our fair community," he said. "Each and every one of you is a hero to us. And I might add your remarkable journey overseas wouldn't have happened if it wasn't for a newcomer to our community—a fellow we once thought could be pushed around on the ice. I'm talking about Clarence Clarington-Clarke, folks. Well, he sure proved he's got iron in his veins and an iron will to match. Thank you, Clarence."

"Now, team, step forward and receive a little gift we have for each of you. Mr. Len Levy, owner of Levy Jewellers, has donated a fancy wristwatch for each of you. Mr. Levy, will you please come up on stage and help make the presentations?"

Len Levy, a shy, middle-aged man, came forward and smiled broadly at each player and the coach as he presented the watches. They were engraved simply "Champions: 1936."

Before leaving the stage, Mr. Levy turned to the Mayor.

"Your Honour, may I take another moment to say something?"

"By all means, Mr. Levy. But don't be long. There's music and dancing to follow. The boys can time your speech on their new watches."

Len Levy smiled and took the microphone.

"Ladies and gentlemen," he began. "I want to say to the players who helped save a young boy from the cruelties of Nazi Germany how grateful we are in the Jewish community..." He paused. "I guess that community consists only of me and my wife, Helga. Anyway, if there's no objection, we would like to volunteer our home as a safe haven for young Alan Ball. We have no children of our own and it seems to me it's as if Alan was destined to join us here in Indian River—almost like a miracle." He turned his sad eyes on Alan. "Alan, it is your choice, of course. But we would feel blessed to have you join us in our home. Please give us that chance."

The crowd erupted in cheering. The applause was sustained. Alan looked at Max, not sure what to do or what to say.

"Mr. Levy is just about the kindest man you'll ever meet," Max said. "And his wife is wonderful."

Alan walked slowly across the stage and put his arms around Mr. Levy's waist. Mrs. Levy ran up on stage and embraced Alan. She was sobbing.

Alan shyly took the microphone, bending it to

meet his height.

"Ladies, gentlemen," he said quietly. "Excuse my accent, please. But I love to move in with Mr. and Mrs. Levy." He began to cry and pulled a handkerchief from his pocket to dab at his eyes. Then he continued.

"Thank you, Max and Marty. You will always be my big brothers. Someday I hope play hockey with you. Skate like you, and knock people down like big Clarence. Thank you, people. All of you my new friends."

Tears were flowing down every cheek before he turned away, once more to be embraced by the Levys, who led him off the stage.

At the dance that followed, the Shelter Valley Boys supplied the music and the merrymaking went on into the night. Clarence won the attention of many of the young women and was a sought-after dance partner. Marty too, showed no hesitation in bouncing to the music with a number of attractive young girls.

Max and Trudy danced together for ten, 20, 40 minutes nonstop.

"The hockey season is finally over," Max said. "I never thought it would end like this, Trudy. And I'm so happy you helped make it a success."

"You're the one who convinced Coach Kennedy to give me a chance," Trudy replied. "When I'm old and gray, I'll never forget this season. And what you did for me." She put her head on his shoulder and sighed. "It'll be something to tell my grand-children."

"Grandchildren!" Max said, pulling back to look Trudy in the face. "Isn't it a little early to be talking about grandchildren?"

"Perhaps. First I'll need to have children of my own."

Max laughed. "How many?"

"Two. Two boys."

"And their names?"

Trudy giggled. "Max and Marty."

"Really?"

She leaned into him. "Really," she whispered. "But first I'll need a mate. Not just a teammate or a linemate—but a life-mate."

She locked eyes with Max and gave him a dazzling smile.

THE REST OF THE STORY

Max and Marty spent the next month writing weekly articles for the *Review* about their season of surprises and their exciting trip to Europe. Max did most of the writing, while Marty supplied several photos he'd taken.

Trudy spent the summer months training and driving harness horses. Her favourite—and the fastest trotter—was Wizard, winner of the previous year's Hambletonian.

Hack Riddell and Ollie Oliver made headlines in July when they attempted to rob a bank in the city. Hack handed the teller a note demanding cash. The note was written on the back of an envelope. They made their escape, but Hack had failed to notice his home address was marked on the front of the envelope. He and Oliver were arrested later that day and were sentenced to lengthy jail terms.

Steve Kennedy and Clarence worked well together at the Gray Paper Mill, and profits showed an immediate improvement. In mid-summer, Kennedy was offered a coaching job with a minor-league pro team, but he declined, stating, "I prefer to stay where I am, working at the mill and coaching my juniors."

Lester Patrick sent Clarence an invitation to join the New York Rangers at training camp. He attended and was offered a contract—but with a Rangers farm team. "No thanks," he told Mr. Patrick. "I can earn more money at the mill back home. Besides, I love my job. I guess I'll play hockey—but just for the fun of it."

Rudi Ball came to town to visit his nephew Alan. He wanted to thank the Mitchell brothers for helping Alan get to North America and the Levys for adopting him and providing him with a wonderful home. (Rudi—and this part is true—later became one of the most popular hockey players in Europe. He played for many years on the German National Team and scored more than 500 career goals. He moved to South Africa in 1948 and died in Johannesburg in 1975. He was inducted into the International Hockey Hall of Fame in 2004.)

James Taylor was fired by the Hartley Wolverines over the summer, after government investigators discovered he had failed to properly file his income tax returns.

Charlie Chin proudly hung a blown-up photo of the Indians on a wall of the family restaurant—the Golden Dragon.

Molly Bright slimmed down to 200 pounds and won both the women's discuss toss and the shot put in the North Country track and field championships.

Other than that, not much happened in Indian River after the hockey season ended. It's a pretty quiet place.